The Two of Us

The Two of Us

Kathy Page

A JOHN METCALF BOOK

BIBLIOASIS
WINDSOR, ONTARIO

FIRST EDITION

Library and Archives Canada Cataloguing in Publication

Page, Kathy, 1958-, author
The two of us / Kathy Page.

Short stories.
Issued in print and electronic formats.
ISBN 978-1-77196-099-1 (paperback).--ISBN 978-1-77196-100-4 (ebook)

I. Title.

PR6066.A325T86 2016 823'.914 C2016-901848-2
C2016-901849-0

Edited by John Metcalf
Copy-edited by Jessica Faulds
Typeset by Chris Andrechek
Cover designed by David Drummond

Canada Council for the Arts
Conseil des Arts du Canada

Canadian Heritage
Patrimoine canadien

Published with the generous assistance of the Canada Council for the Arts and the Ontario Arts Council. Biblioasis also acknowledges the support of the Government of Canada through the Canada Book Fund and the Government of Ontario through the Ontario Book Publishing Tax Credit.

PRINTED AND BOUND IN CANADA

MIX
Paper from responsible sources
FSC® C004071

Contents

The House on Manor Close

Loganberries

WE ATE FROM PALE GREEN plates on an oval table in a square dining room adjoining the kitchen and linked to it by a sliding door. The French windows that led from the dining room to the garden were often steamed up, blurring the view. A shaded lamp suspended above the table rose and fell smoothly when you pushed or pulled the little handle beneath the bulb.

My father's seat at the head of the table faced the back garden, its lawns, trees and banks of flowering shrubs so bright in summer that they almost hurt your eyes.

Mum's place was opposite Dad, but most of the time she was in the kitchen, where she prepared every morsel that passed our lips and washed every dish, cup, knife, fork and table napkin that we ever used. She even buttered our bread for us and decided whether or not our toast would have crusts: this was the custom of the time, and quite unremarkable. On the other hand, although we sat down together at the table, we rarely ate the same meal, which was not.

While my father ate a pork chop with boiled cabbage and new potatoes, my older sister Julia and I might have cold chicken and lettuce with salad cream, and my mother a pork pie, beetroot, of which she was particularly fond, and peas. Occasionally there was one element—perhaps the potatoes, peas or beans from the garden—that featured in all the meals, linking them tenuously together. But mostly there was not.

On the kitchen side of the table sat the oldest of us three girls, Julia—officially Juliette, but adamantly opposed to the name's romantic implications. I, Hazel, named after a tree planted on the weekend of my birth, sat opposite her, my back against the heating vent in the living room wall. April, still a baby, was fed earlier and then "put down."

Plates were handed out from the kitchen and my mother told us what was coming and who it was for. If your plate contained something you were known to like, then you were in her good books, and it was important to seem grateful even though fried eggs might be the last thing on earth you fancied at that particular moment. If you were given something you had even once shown the faintest dislike for, she was either punishing you or reminding you that she could. We never argued over what we were given, though occasionally we attempted to exchange—beetroot for potato, sausage for chop. Mum said that what bothered her about this was the possibility of the tablecloth getting spoiled. Sometimes, unable to contain herself, she would pull the plates from our hands and perform the exchange herself, insisting that the entire meal was swapped so that you got three things you didn't want along with the one you did. "Don't fiddle about!" she said.

This was in suburbia, before the arrival of the avocado pear, and again, the food itself—meat, pies, potatoes, boiled vegetables and rudimentary but very fresh salads from the garden—was, in name at least, ordinary. But there were many staple items which Mum had never learned to successfully make. Yorkshire pudding was one, pastry another. These substances were different every time they appeared and could only be named from their context. Sometimes the Yorkshire pudding resembled scrambled egg, at other times it was more like a large, thick crisp. There was no way of predicting.

"What's it like?" she'd ask. Neither I nor Julia answered, but my father had grown into the habit of considering the merits of whatever it was very carefully indeed and making a considered reply.

"I quite like the softness of it. I must say it goes extremely well with mustard."

The reason for the inconsistency was simple. Despite her rigorousness in other areas of household management, such as cleaning and expenditure, Mum hated to be bound by measurements or recipes. She preferred to guess and she despised recipes for being so particular, so fussy about what they needed to be themselves. She simply wouldn't accept it and gave them, as she gave us, what she thought they deserved.

About once a year something new would make its way into the repertoire.

"It said egg whites," she would explain as she served it, "but there wasn't quite enough flour and I couldn't find the separator so I halved the number and used whole eggs. I don't like vanilla so I changed it for cinnamon and I just didn't bother with the pears."

"The custardy bit is nice," Dad responded, cautiously, while we all watched him. "What is it called, then?"

It didn't really matter what he said, because my mother would only make whatever it was again if she herself had enjoyed it—and even if she had, and repeated the dish, it would not be the same the second time around, not even remotely *like*.

I knew, from visits and from television, that this wasn't the way other families did things. When grown-up guests came, I stared at my water glass as the plates were handed out.

"You and Michael have got pork," I'd hear my Mum say, "but I've done a leg of lamb as well..." Occasionally, she might even offer startled guests a choice, as if we were in a restaurant, though we rarely went to those, for she found the spectacle of our free choice hard to bear and having herself to be on the end of someone else's cuisine more or less impossible.

"I've got three steaks, and the others can have shepherd's pie. Now, which do you want?" Whatever they chose, Mum would extol the merits of the *other* thing, and make them change their minds. The guests hid their bewilderment behind stretched smiles and tended to leave as soon as Mum had loudly undertaken the extensive washing up and brought out the coffee. Everyone got that, though those who asked for it black often found themselves with cream.

I loved to visit my own friends' homes, where the contents of everyone's plates looked identical (except that the men always had more), and if you said you liked something they gave you another helping and made sure to have it the next time you visited. My unusual enthusiasm at the table made me a sought-after guest, but this entailed "having them back," which was first an ordeal and then a revelation: I watched, mesmerized, as Sonia Brotherton slipped the whole of something wet and leathery, which Mum called *quiche,* into her shorts pocket. Occasionally I had considered refusing to eat this or that but it had always seemed more trouble than it was worth. Now the solution was apparent. On the way back to her house, Sonia posted the quiche into a letterbox.

"Your mum's crazy, you know," she said, matter-of-fact, wiping her hands on her tee-shirt. I grinned, shrugged, suspecting that things were actually far worse than that, that we were all crazy, or if not, soon would be.

At Sonia's home her mother sat us on stools in the kitchen and gave us each a little glass bowl of halved strawberries topped with a twist of whipped cream and sugar fine as dust; they tasted heavenly and I ate so slowly, savouring them, that she asked twice whether I was feeling all right.

The morning after this, I pushed my plate of baked beans (which Mum had told me needed using up) to one side.

"I don't really fancy beans, Mum," I said. "I'd rather have cornflakes." Julia, opposite me, had those. Next to me, April, enthroned in her high chair, was smearing her face with mashed banana. My father had been served with All-Bran as well as beans on brown toast. My mother, opposite him at the far end of the table, was eating a piece of white toast topped with lemon curd. Her face slackened. She stopped chewing and stood. I realized belatedly that Sonia Brotherton and I were not in the same position because she went home to somewhere else, whereas I lived here, but I had begun something fateful and could only continue. "You can't make me!" I said, sick with adrenaline.

I had no idea whether this was true. I had dressed for the occasion in a loose skirt with deep pockets. It would not work for beans, but I slipped my hands inside them for comfort as I spoke.

The truth was that sometimes my mother could make me eat and sometimes she couldn't. But whether or not she could did not greatly matter because from that moment on, for many years to come, what did or did not go in my mouth was to be the entire focus of both our lives, and the only subject of our conversation:

"I don't like it."

"It's what there is. It's good for you."

"I don't want it."

"Eat it."

This interminable argument was largely ignored by the rest of the family. Julia, a decade older than me, was increasingly away from home. April benefitted from the lack of attention. My father did occasionally protest, setting down his cutlery to ask the space in front of him whether it was too much to ask that a man might eat in peace? Afterwards, he would be served for his next meal something he was known to abhor, such as cheese on toast or a semi-liquid omelette. He would often try to skip the meal after that.

"You're giving your father indigestion!" my mother said.

I could not stop, and neither could she.

I grew hollow-limbed and paper-thin. There was, back then, no name for what was happening.

And in contrast to the hollowness inside me, I felt the weight and solidity of the house on Manor Close, its brick and tile and parquet, its accumulated wardrobes, bedsteads, sideboards, dining table and chairs bearing down, crushing me. I fled outdoors. Craving light and freedom, I paced intricate routes out through suburban streets, cycled out to the edges of the countryside, or lay on my back, hidden in the hedged area at the far end of the garden where roses grew in a circular bed. The air was threaded with rustlings and songs, and gradually I began to see the birds as well as hear them. Chaffinches and blue tits that skittered from twig to twig, screeching jays, bold robins, thrushes and blackbirds… I bought a bird book and a sketch pad. The birds and their behaviours filled my mind and even worked their way into my dreams. I envied their lightness and the physical freedom they seemed to enjoy, how they fed and flocked and flew, all together, without argument.

Mum's cheeks developed a high colour and at the same time fell, making her eyes seem to bulge. I learned later that she had two miscarriages during this time. Dad developed an ulcer. April went to play group and began to have friends, but she still followed me everywhere because I was the only one left at home. Julia was in college, then working. Sometimes she brought a boyfriend home to lunch or dinner on the weekend. A guest meant that the struggle between me and my mother would become muted and underhand, though sometimes the guest would be asked his opinion:

"We have such trouble with Hazel and her food! Does that look like 'too much' to you, David?"

"Depends how hungry someone is, I suppose," the innocent boyfriend would say, looking cheerfully about the room.

My father would engage the young man in conversation.

"I hear you're interested in history?" he might begin, and then ask with false jocularity, "Who was it, now, who said, 'History is a philosophy from examples'?"

"I'm not sure..." the boyfriend would reply, chewing perplexedly on his Yorkshire pudding, whilst Dad carefully loaded a fork with meat and greens, glanced up, judged the length of the pause.

"Dionysius of Halicarnassus, 30 to 7 BC," he would eventually pronounce, then fill his mouth with the loaded forkful and say nothing more for the duration of the meal. He kept the *Oxford Dictionary of Quotations* in the garden shed and prepared carefully each time a new boyfriend was invited. But Julia was no fool and soon learned to avoid bringing the conventional or oversensitive to our table, which now included April, a very messy eater prone to offering guests morsels from her plate. Julia took to strong men, humourists, louts who weren't interested in anything and so could not be humiliated, or, alternatively, men with such monolithic confidence in themselves that nothing could shatter it. She also took to miniskirts, and on one occasion wore a transparent blouse to Sunday lunch.

My parents ignored this, but I, placed next to April and opposite Julia and the current boyfriend (who was of the arrogant type—a thin, monosyllabic artist), stared intently through the film of white chiffon. I hadn't really seen nipples before, and hers, in our unheated dining room, were large as loganberries. I could not take my eyes away.

Looking at them, I somehow knew that one day my life would be something bigger than whether I could get away without eating my supper or not. One day I too would have breasts, though I wasn't sure whether they should be as large, as absolutely round and moulded-looking as my sister's. At the neck of the blouse was a white ruff, and above it, her face, flushed from the wine, was made up with dark eyeliner and silver on the lids. She had the same silver on her nails and had taken to eating everything with just a fork. She was nothing like the angry, jealous girl who had accused me of being Mum's favourite and, to punish me, removed the tree-house ladder, leaving me stranded.

Hopefully, once I too left, I would be nothing like me. I would go to university and become a scientist. I would travel the world and see exotic birds. One day, however distant, I would never have to sit at this table again, nor look at the apple-green cloth with the lacy holes in it, nor the pale green wallpaper, nor the even greener garden beyond the French windows, full of birds I could not quite see because of the condensation and because my mother blocked my view. One day, I would recover my appetite. I would eat in restaurants. I would eat interesting, pretty-looking food that fitted its name: iced pear sabayon, ceviche, oeufs en cocotte, mouselline de poisson, soupe au pistou, roast carp with peppers, quail's egg salad, daube à la provencale, iced borscht with cumin, veal blanquette, blinis, pasta alla carbonara, blackcurrant kissel, cinnamon cheesecake, coeur à la crème—all of it and more. I would sit in a muted atmosphere of whispers and clinking glass, while a fan whirred away above my head and a tall waiter stood patiently beside me as I, very slowly, made up my mind.

Julia's eyes met mine and I became the loganberries: I blushed purple-red. Back in tree-house days, she would have said something to embarrass me. Now, she smiled.

Wonder

I, the baby, April, sometimes known as "Ape," hardly knew my eldest sister, Julia, and although I desperately wanted to love Hazel, she ignored me and cared only for birds. She won prizes for her bird drawings, which she did in a firm outline, head pointing to the left, and then filled in with watercolour. Beneath, she printed the common and proper names, the season and a sign for male or female and signed her name, Hazel Seymour. When she used drawing pins to display these drawings on the walls of her room, turning them into a sky as overpopulated as a summer beach, my mother did not punish her for ruining the walls, though she scolded me for laughing at Hazel when she stuck her head between the railings of Palmerston Park to watch the mandarin ducks. The fire brigade had to come and saw her free.

Hazel was thin, fine-boned, with red cheeks and small but glistening brown eyes. When she wasn't talking about birds, she was silent, or absent. She sat for hours in the garden, motionless and bundled in sweaters, her field guide, notebook and pencil at the ready. Occasionally there was a yellowhammer or a bullfinch, though mostly she just noted common birds like chaffinches and robins, in all their ages and stages. Her ears, tuned to their calls, filtered out our voices.

She argued constantly with my mother over coming in for dinner or lunch, and not eating when she did, and she made me feel terrible for eating chicken and always being hungry. She was saving her pocket money for binoculars. When she grew up she would be an ornithologist.

Hazel loved birds and I, unable to break through but unwilling to give up, observed this passion of hers. I saw that love could not be done by halves. Nor was it rational, or fair. It demanded dedication, as did its opposite, hate. Our mother hated germs and fought them daylong. They had to be prevented from getting in our mouths or noses, and the important thing was not to touch either of these places, but in case we forgot, we had to wash our hands with amber-coloured see-through soap to kill them. Germs came out of your bottom and crept through the paper as you wiped yourself. All of us were chronically constipated. Germs were in the grass, so we always wore shoes outdoors. By the back step stood a little bowl of milky disinfectant and a scrubbing brush for us to clean the soles. My parents shared a passion for the garden, and Mum donned gardening gloves for the simplest outdoor task, then afterwards rinsed them and left them to dry outside. The rest of us were supposed to do the same, but forgot.

Anything new that came indoors was washed straight away, even if it was sealed in plastic. Daily Mum scoured the kitchen with bleach, including the walls. Animals were prime carriers of germs, due to sniffing themselves, and so naturally none were allowed in. In our house, things you touched were nearly always damp from just having been wiped.

I was dreamy. Hazel was clever and did very well at school. I learned from her that germs were also what made you have a baby. They came from the man and got in the woman if she wasn't careful. Also, she said, I was an accident, by which I understood some failure on the cleaning front. She always got top marks. Mr. Leaper told my mother she was a born scientist and could easily go to university. Everyone encouraged her.

Dad was for years designing Hazel a cat-proof bird table, though he never completed it. He often didn't finish things, and the shed was full of abandoned projects, but perhaps in this case it was also because in his heart he felt creatures should be kept in their place—which was the farmyard or on the dinner plate—and because he loved the garden and hated both pigeons, which might use the bird table if he actually finished it, and cats and dogs. One passion necessitates or modifies another. He covered the raspberries and peas in fine green net, and the garden was kept dog-proof by tall fences and barbed wire threaded through the hedges. But there was nothing you could do about cats except chase them.

Hazel disliked cats too, but hated even more the disturbance caused by chasing them. At mealtimes, she kept her notepad by her plate. She craned her neck and fixed her eyes on what she could see of the garden, and I in turn watched her as she counted and marked, occasionally picking at her food, a morsel here, a morsel there. I began to think that when she grew up she would become not an ornithologist but an actual bird. I wanted her to fly away. I was jealous, something else that can't be done by halves.

*

The green woodpecker was an astonishing bird, with ringed eyes and a red patch on its head, like a skullcap. It was shivering and had a broken wing, and Hazel had found it in a hedge, wrapped it in her cardigan and carried it home. She wanted to bring it *in*. I stood beside my mother on the threshold and waited to see what would happen. Mum's face was tight, her lips sealed, her breath held against the germ-laden air. She wiped her hands up and down on her apron. I watched as Hazel's dark eyes sought my mother's pale grey ones and tugged at them, half pleading, half imperious.

"*Picus Viridis*," she announced, "I want to keep it in my room—" adding, "I can make it better. A scientific experiment." My mother's hands fell still. None of us breathed.

"I suppose so," she replied, "if you wipe it down."

How very much my mother loved Hazel—even more than she hated germs! I watched my sister wipe the green woodpecker gently with disinfectant, and then carry it up to her room.

Shortly after this, I won two goldfish in a fair and brought them home in a plastic bag, my heart swollen, my stomach brimful and fragile like the bag. It was, I knew, some kind of test. But as I stood on the tiled doorstep, I felt my eyes sliding away from my mother's, even as I tried to magic her the way Hazel had. Fish were not animals, I insisted, and besides, it was only *fair*. I wanted to have the fish in a tank in my bedroom, like my sister and her green woodpecker. But, Mum insisted in return, it was not the same. The fish were not sick, and no one had said I was a born scientist. Also, it was difficult to see how to wipe them.

"I'll ask your father if you can keep them in the garden," she decided.

Underneath the red-leaved tree my father called *Prunus*, a tank was covered with wire that went right over the top and down the sides and was then tucked in under some old bricks. This was to stop cats, and foxes. The foxes came at night. You heard them shriek to each other and you might catch a sight of them trotting up the path if the moon was out. Sometimes I dreamed of the foxes, pawing and nosing at the bricks that held the mesh on the tank in place. I dreamed of finding an empty tank and two white skeletons, sucked clean, on the bright green lawn. I loved my fish. I didn't draw them. I just looked.

Hazel's room became a bird hospital. It had a sign on the door: "Birds: Do Not Disturb," and a large bowl of milky disinfectant outside. The patients, finches and thrushes, blackbirds, even storm gulls, were arranged in shoebox rows. Broken limbs were set with splints and sticking plaster. Diets were prescribed and administered. She served them pipettes of milk-soaked bread, live worms. Some birds lived. Those who died were buried in their shoeboxes in the back right-hand corner of the garden, a shady corner where nothing but ground ivy would grow. Hazel, busy with her avian hospital, forgave my mother for her cooking and began to eat again. She became kinder to me, too.

Occasionally I was allowed to enter the bird hospital, leaving behind me the dust-free carpets, gleaming mouldings and wiped light fixtures of the rest of the house. In Hazel's room the sills were dull with dust, the carpet peppered with crumbs. Rimed saucers and jars of desiccated worms stood on the bedside table, and the counterpane was blobbed and streaked with droppings. I held the birds, wrapped in cloth, while Hazel bathed their eyes or tapped at their beaks with the pipette until they opened wide. She still drew. The pictures now showed birds in all sorts of positions—preening, nestled together, poised at takeoff or landing, pointing both right and left.

The room was dark, to keep the birds calm and help them to forget about flying. But when they began to eat better, to peck and flap and flutter about, the curtains would be opened and the windows flung wide. Perhaps immediately, perhaps days later, the bird would suddenly hop to the sill, then soar into the sky. You could tell when it had happened because afterwards Hazel's eyes glistened with satisfaction, as if, I thought to myself, she had laid an egg. She was doing biology at school by then, and did indeed eventually go on to university—an education that finally enabled her to refute our mother's belief that all germs were necessarily bad.

I still went to see my fish in the garden every day. I lay on my stomach and stared at them as they wove between the weeds, sucked their food from the water's skin or simply hung suspended in a kind of fishy sleep. Time stretched and shrunk and passed. Inside, in a row on my bed, I had animal toys. A panda bear, an owl, a kangaroo, a lion, all with button eyes. I almost loved them but I knew there was a difference between the living and the stuffed, between wonder and comfort. Between humans and animals, animals and birds, birds and fish, which lived where people couldn't even breathe. They had only glass to hold them from a poisonous world. Maybe it was cruel to keep them, but now I could not be without their swimming gold and their sudden, swivelling eyes. Looking at them was somehow looking inside me, at a part I didn't understand, a secret and a miracle. It must, I thought, be the same for Hazel with her birds. I forgave her. I reasoned that if she was right about my mother's accident with the germs, then she was one as well.

That winter, it snowed and my fish tank froze overnight to a solid block of white ice. I trudged through the snow to visit it every day, as people visit graves. Dumb with reproach, I refused to allow it to be disposed of. When the thaw came, I watched the ice melt day by day, revealing a small golden glow at the very heart. I felt sadder and sadder, as if I was melting too. And then, as I watched, the two fish moved, slowly at first, as if waking from a long, cold dream.

The Garden Path

Their faces grew leathery, tanned, blotched; their eyes saw distance well but not things that were close up. They stopped reading and spent more and more time in their garden, which soon became the only subject of their conversations. Dad, completely bald, wore a brown corduroy cap to protect him from the sun. Mum's hair, always unmanageable, now thinning and unevenly mixed between grey and white, surrounded her face in tufts and wisps. She abandoned her fortnightly visits to the hairdresser: the style would be lost as soon as a bit of wind touched her. "Besides, Juliette," she said, "who sees us?"

I saw them often because I lived the nearest. Single again, I had ended up in a warehouse conversion forty minutes' drive away. My flat was on the third floor and had a tiny balcony with space for two wrought iron chairs and a matching table, upon which sat the series of ill-fated potted geraniums that Mum persisted in giving me. I had secure parking and there was a gym in the basement. I liked it a lot.

"Gardening is far better than artificial exercise," Mum told me. "Remember how Alex Rawlings suddenly went kaput, even after all those hours he spent sweating on that stationery bike of his. Though hygiene is very important too, of course."

First light would find my father, in his dressing gown, rubber gardening shoes and thick-rimmed spectacles, inspecting the roses for aphids, or, if it had rained overnight, checking the level in the water butts. He would feel how the peaches espaliered on the south wall held to their stalks, and carefully pick any that were ripe. Slowly, he would crouch down and tug the beginnings of a dandelion from the lawn. An hour later they both sat, dressed in loose trousers and old cotton shirts, in the small summer house my father had erected during the second year of his retirement. This was the time to drink strong tea and decide what the day's work would be.

I had to admit that both they and the garden were thriving, and yet adding more beds, more work, more commitment, was an odd thing to do at their age, counterintuitive.

"Things take a bit longer than they used to," Dad

admitted, "but we have so much more time, now that we're no longer responsible for anything else."

"Cooking is far simpler for just the two of us," Mum pointed out.

They took to travelling abroad in winter and returned with lists. They smuggled seeds, bulbs or cuttings, the root ends wrapped in damp tissue paper and bits of plastic bag. The rest of the year they stayed at home. Even so, I learned never to phone them in the daytime. They would be at the Far End, as it was called, kneeling to weed the circular rose bed, or in the Front Patch, or ventilating the compost heaps, or raking leaves. On a chilly evening, they'd be out wrapping delicate shrubs to save them from the frost, or carrying pots into the conservatory they had added at the back of the house.

"It's wonderful," my father told me, "to have the opportunity to be completely taken over."

Several years passed this way and then, at the end of the supper I cooked in my flat to celebrate the tenth anniversary of my father's retirement, he leaned forward and said, "Julia, I don't like to bring this up, but suppose that one day we can't manage the garden properly?"

"We couldn't bear to see it neglected," Mum added, and helped herself to more supermarket raspberries and cream, despite having earlier complained that they were tasteless.

They told me the familiar story of how they, she in her twenties, he thirty, just married, had moved into a large flat in London. A Victorian building with high ceilings and huge windows, it overlooked a park and all around were gardens. From behind their windows my parents watched the first postwar summer erupt into bloom. They knew they were lucky to have so much space in the midst of an accommodation shortage, yet they watched other people all around them digging and planting and were surprised to find themselves discontented. The landlady downstairs had a garden, and Mum was given permission to hang her laundry in it twice a week, but only that. She could not sit there, she could not so much as scratch the earth or plant a single seed. And so my mother discovered that she wanted a garden—not just a small city plot, but a real garden—that she yearned for it more than anything else. Soon, it was the same for my father.

They moved to a new suburb. The land surrounding the brand new house—the would-be garden—had once been the grounds of a manor house, and was now a mass of nettles, mud and broken brick. They bought a wheelbarrow, tools, grass seed, gardening books, and pamphlets outlining the correct way to dig. They carted the rubble away bit by bit, laid paths, mapped out borders, planted trees. Almost coincidentally, or even, perhaps, accidentally, I was born. By the time I was a toddler, labour in the garden was strictly divided. My father dug, sprayed, dealt with trees and hedges and vegetables, spread manure, mowed the lawn and had complete control of the vegetable plot. My mother, who had special gardening outfits and rituals to do with shoes and gloves, harvested, weeded the non-vegetable areas, pruned, and patted in bedding plants.

Busy with their plants, they let ten years slip by before they had Hazel, and another seven before April. Each of us only briefly intersected with the others and grew up more or less separately, and then, one by one, we left. I was the first to leave Manor Close, but after a spell in the Midlands, then Brussels, I came back to the southeast for work. Hazel spent years travelling and then eventually settled on a hillside in Cumbria: wonderful views, great birds, and just about as far north as is possible to go whilst remaining in the country. April, the freest of us all, outdid her by crossing the Atlantic.

They both had families, whereas I've done better at jobs than at long-term relationships. I was middle-aged, free of dependents, close and available—and there, in my glittering and scarcely-used kitchen sat my parents, my admittedly difficult parents, who had become two sweet old people wanting me to help them with their garden.

They studied each other across the table, conspiratorial.

"So why not get someone in to cut the lawn and trim the hedges?" I suggested. They could afford help. If they were unwilling to pay, I would.

"Oh," my father said, "I've seen those chaps. Butchers. Not one of them does a proper job."

"The garden is a personal, well, a *family* thing—"

"There must be someone," I said. "Lots of people have their grass cut." I collected the bowls, racked them in my dishwasher.

"Really, we'd rather *move* than see someone mess it up."

"We wondered," Dad began, "if it came to it, whether you'd be able..." He let the sentence trail. Mum, I knew, had set him up for this, for the fantasy of me spending my weekends on my knees, grovelling in the undergrowth according to their directions.

"I love the garden," I said, drying my hands. "But you know I've never really liked *gardening*. Maybe you could somehow simplify it."

"Simplify?" Mum said, her eyes very bright. "I remember how you used to be jealous of the garden," she added.

It was true. My parents never seemed to want to *play*. They spent entire weekends kneeling, collecting debris in mounds, preparing seedbeds or disinfecting the greenhouse. At the end of the day they would walk around, examining each other's work, and then, after a cold supper, they fell asleep in their armchairs. Then it was the week again, with everyone back to work or school.

They gave me a small area of garden, offered me surplus plants and cuttings to put in as I chose, along with endless advice. I tried, but it did not interest me. Plants did not talk. They took ages to take, even longer to get big; they were prone to rot, insect invasion, desiccation, wilt. My fingers were clumsy. Pretending to tend the soil, I lost myself in hopes for buried treasure or Roman remains, and for a brother or a sister. I collected worms, kept them in flowerpots, forgot to water them, wept when I found the brittle remains.

Eventually they reclaimed my patch. I resolved that that when I left home I would live somewhere as far away from greenery as possible, and not visit much. Though actually, during my second divorce, out of desperation, I stayed with my parents for an entire fortnight.

"Sit in the garden, dear," Mum had said, then. "Look at those azaleas! They will do you good." The colours were extraordinary and intense; I understood that it was the very best she could think of, but stayed resolutely in the living room, with the curtains drawn over the picture windows, the telephone to one side of me, a box of tissues to the other.

So, no, the garden could not be simplified, and I would not say yes. My father put his hand over my mother's.

I switched on the dishwasher, brewed some decaf. If they did have to move, my parents explained as they drank it, their swollen hands dwarfing my delicate silver-rimmed cups, they weren't sure how they would feel about having a smaller garden, about having to start all over again.

It was all unimaginable. Even in my home, where they had been many times before, they looked out of place. The pair of them sat side by side, apple-cheeked, windswept, like two peasants who had strayed into a smart café.

"Maybe it would be best to have no garden at all," my father said, not meaning it.

"It hasn't happened yet," I told them, and poured us each a small brandy. My hand shook a little, but they didn't see. We drank to their garden, and that night I dreamed of it gone wild, its fences collapsed and lawns neglected, the shrubbery rampant, the flowerbeds thick with weeds and shaded by huge shaggy trees.

I reported all this to Hazel and April. We fretted for a week or two, but found no answers and abandoned the conversation.

"The *Fremontodendron* is doing well," Dad said one time over the small whiskies we often drank when I came to visit, after dusk, always, unless I wanted to help. Even at that hour, it was obligatory to take a tour, and indeed the flowers seemed particularly beautiful in the blue half-light, their colours glowing in a deep, mysterious way.

"That's lovely," I said, "that one with the white flowers and the scent."

"*Abelia triflora*," he told me. "You gave us that for our last anniversary."

"Show her the *Dendromecon*!" Mum called from the patio.

Their vocabularies still increased daily. I could not keep up.

Time went on passing, but all the signs were that they were immortal, that this was their June. They would reach midsummer—and then just continue. The days would not diminish; instead, they would lengthen until there was no night left. The plants would grow huge and my father and mother, wrinkled, copper-brown, would move from towering bush to bursting border carrying their forks and spades, their bits of twine and secateurs, dwarfed by what they grew. It would all just go on forever until the dahlias were as big as houses and they were as small as ants, just part of the thing they had made... I see now that this was denial, of course, but in the year when my mother turned seventy-nine and my father eighty-four, they were still strong and the garden had never looked so good.

I bought them a cellphone. Mostly, of course, they forgot, or took it out, then lost it in the shrubbery and had to call it from their landline and walk around the garden, listening. I hunted down a gardening apron with a special Velcro pocket to keep the phone in. When the accident happened, Mum was wearing it and had the phone with her. She was able to call the ambulance quickly, but twenty-five minutes later, it still had not arrived. She called me. I was in a departmental meeting but they put her through: Dad had fallen from a ladder when pulling bindweed from the yew hedge at the back. She had been watering the patio and had heard nothing, but, sensing that something was wrong, went to look, and found him on the ground.

"It's his leg. His hip—Juliette, I called half an hour ago!" she cried. "They haven't come!"

I called the ambulance again, and drove as fast as I could to Manor Close. The sprinkler was full on in the middle of the front lawn, throwing water into the bright air. I ran through the side gate, under its arch of wisteria, past the peach tree heavy with fruit and straight up the path to the hedge. The ladder was there on the grass, and next to it, the cellphone. They had gone. To St Mary's or the General? I called both hospitals, each of which said they would call me right back to confirm whether or not my father had been admitted.

Long minutes passed. It was my fault. No, it was not. Not exactly. *This damn garden,* I remember thinking. Still my phone did not ring and I did not know where to go or what to do. I walked out onto the brick patio, bordered by beds of delphiniums, aquilegia and digitalis. The sound of bees was everywhere, and it grew particularly loud as I approached the massive *Buddleja globosa* which they had planted only a few years ago. There was a bee on almost every spherical bloom and a thick, distracting smell.

If my call wasn't returned in the next five minutes, I told myself, I would set off for St Mary's. Meanwhile, I walked up the garden path. To the right, *Clematis florida 'Sieboldii'* grew around what once had been my childhood swing, and the patch of ground that had been mine, no longer shaded, was home to a regiment of bearded irises, fierce violet against the almost unnaturally green lawn. Beyond, I could see beds of azaleas and the rowan tree, and beyond that the dark yew hedge itself. Just in front of that stood huge laburnum, which had come to my shoulder when I was a girl and now towered thirty feet above my head. To the left was the vegetable patch, now much reduced but still backed by the espaliered pear trees, all different varieties, arranged in sequence of their time of fruiting with the earliest nearest to the house. The soil was a rich, chocolate brown. Leaves thrust and shimmered in an infinite variety of flagrant and subtle greens; birds poured out their songs, and insects flitted and drifted through the warm, moist air.

Just before my phone rang, I noticed a dandelion, its flowers on the verge of opening, at the edge of the lawn. Before I knew it (and as if someone other than me was willing it), I hitched up my skirt, crouched down, thrust my fingers into the soil, and tugged. The taproot broke and my fingers burrowed deeper, grasped it again and eased out the pale, grubby thing. The mouldy smell of disturbed soil and the intricate scents of pollen and chlorophyll blended into an irresistible cocktail of sweetness and decay.

The Last Cut

WINTER SUNLIGHT STREAMED in through the plate-glass windows at the front of the salon; it was early still, and Eric's new client, Cara—naturally chestnut, ivory skin—sat swathed in a black cape, watching him in the mirror as he sectioned her hair. Her lips were immaculately rouged, her nails polished to match, and the boots that poked out from beneath the black cape presented a perfect blend of quirky and chic. A copy of *Vogue* was spread across her lap.

"So sorry to interrupt," the receptionist murmured, holding out the phone. "It's Renée's client, Mrs. Swenson. She says she can't wait until next week."

Renée had spoken to Eric about Mrs. Swenson before she left. He took the call over by the desk, adjusting the arrangement of fresh stargazer lilies as he spoke.

"She explained the situation to me. She was terribly sorry that she had to cancel your appointment. A family matter—she had no choice."

"Understood. But the thing is," Mrs. Swenson replied, "I need it done." Mrs. Swenson was one of Renée's regulars, but Eric had once or twice cut her hair, which he remembered she wore in a knot at the back. She was maintenance, rather than style, middle-aged, very low-key. And now this. He adopted a soothing tone, promised to contact her if an earlier appointment became available, and explained that, in any case, Renée would be back in a few days.

"I need it done *today*," she told him.

"We're fully booked," he said, and heard a gasp at the other end. "But perhaps one of the juniors—"

"Please," Mrs. Swenson said, her voice quiet now, but all the more insistent. "Please. Would *you* do the deed? I don't mind how late."

"But surely you'd be more comfortable with a woman?"

"I know you," she told him, and he could not refuse.

Back at the mirror, he apologized profusely, misted Cara's hair, unclipped the top section, combed, then paused with the scissors poised.

"You're sure?" A brief nod: she was absolutely certain.

He liked that, and he liked the way she watched his hands go about their work—interested, expecting the best. No anxiety. He knew already that she could carry off the bold asymmetrical cut she'd chosen, and this, for him, was what it was all about: creating a splendid surface that gave pleasure, enhanced the face, drew others in. Something that emphasized the best points of a personality, and served as status symbol—armour, even, if required. The dramatic statement. The perfect product. The finishing touches. *This* he was good at. Not social work. Not—

"Let me guess," he said to Cara. "Media?" Her eyebrows leaped up, a fresh smile formed.

"PR."

"Close."

He might be useless with sickness, crying, or babies, but he could do chat. Also gifts, surprises, places to go. He always knew exactly what to buy for his sisters' kids at birthdays and Christmas: jackpot every time.

"You spend too much," Emma said to him once, taking him aside in the kitchen. "What are you trying to make up for?" She'd put the flat of her hand on his chest. "It's okay. You don't need to."

"I don't know what you mean," he said.

Sprigs of hair gathered around their feet and the junior swept them away. Cara talked about an art gallery event she was organizing, and Eric nodded, his comb gliding through the damp, well-conditioned hair. Periodically, his eyes flicked up to meet hers in the glass. Eight or more hours a day he talked in the mirror like this. After work, if he went straight into some kind of social situation, he missed the mirror, felt at the same time not quite there and overexposed.

Was there something missing in him? Even though he had been busy, he could have gone home—and then to the hospital—more often during his mother's last months. But he hadn't known what to say. He sat by the bed, and within an hour he was desperate, tense with the desire to leave. He didn't like seeing her that way. He felt terrible, sent flowers regularly, the very best.

"Jo and I just did what was in front of us," Emma had said to him, that time in the kitchen. "We were there and glad to do it. You had just bought the salon."

Though he was his mother's favourite, of course. They all knew that.

Short layers on the right. The long swoop to the left.

"It's a really strong structure," he told Cara. "Looks great on you."

His throat and eyes ached. His chest, too. He wished he had found a way to say no to Mrs. Swenson.

He pumped up the chair, combed again, changed scissors and leaned in close, aware of the different sound the new pair made—faint but very sharp and pure. Soon would come the blow-dry and the shoulder brushing, the showing of the back of the head, the nods, smiles, compliments and thanks, the final removal of the cloak. It was silly to let the thought of Mrs. Swenson get in the way of these things, all of which he enjoyed, but it did. He was already thinking that he must check the room at the back, make sure it was properly set up, clean and warm enough. Anger washed over him, then guilt, which he struggled to repudiate: So that's how it is. We're not all the same. What I do is worth *something*.

He reached for the finishing spray. Cara closed her eyes and the air filled with a delicate, rosemary-scented mist.

"There," he told her, and she tossed her head to see the way it moved.

"Perfect!"

At the end of a cut, he liked to shake hands.

He called the number Renée had left. Given the time difference, she was probably in bed, but he left a message just in case she was able to get back to him. He asked Tasha what approach he should take.

"I've never done it," she said. "But at college, they said start from the back, take it bit by bit, and talk a lot. And, Eric, it's obvious, but remember she is feeling worse than you."

At the end of the day he let the others go, checked the till and retrieved Mrs. Swenson's card, upon which Renée had noted her cut and colour (*dark honey*) and a preference for English breakfast tea, with milk. He filled the kettle, and then settled in the leather chair behind the reception desk to read about the spring styles. When he put down the magazine, it was half past six. This whole thing, he thought, as he listened to the ringing tone on Mrs. Swenson's home number—apparently she did not have a cell—could have been more or less over for both of them by now, but no, here he was, in suspended animation; there she was, god knew where. Perhaps she had changed her mind. Perhaps she had forgotten.

"Eric," he told the answering service in a carefully neutral tone, "from Hair Design. Calling at six thirty." He could quite legitimately leave now, but, just as he was considering it, a small woman in a much-too-large coat pushed in through the big glass door.

"I'm afraid we're closed," he said.

"Sorry!" she said in Mrs. Swenson's voice. "I lost my keys. Thank you for waiting."

She surrendered a claret-coloured scarf along with her coat but did not remove the matching beret and kept a tight hold on her canvas tote bag.

"I've set up the room at the back, Mrs. Swenson."

"Please call me Susanna," she said.

In the back room, boxes of stock reared up around them and there was no window, but it was at least warm, well-lit, private.

"Tea?"

"Please."

We will be here until after seven, he thought, as he jiggled the bag in the cup. He felt a little nauseous. When it was done, he promised himself, he would go to the gym, and after that pick up a movie and takeout.

He noticed a faint tremor in her hands as he passed her the tea.

"How long is it, now, that I've been coming here?" she asked.

"Since before I bought the business," he told her. She hadn't yet removed the beret, so he perched on the stool nearby. "You were here when it was still Chez Claire. The whole area's rocketed, hasn't it?"

She sipped, looked back at him. Her eyes were large and clear, though the skin on her face looked dry and inert. It was shocking how little she resembled the person he remembered.

"Thanks for fitting me in. Next week," she said, "after the chemo, I'll be feeling very bad, so it had to be now."

It was every bit as difficult as he'd thought. Every bit. He swallowed back the sour taste in his mouth. If he could have run, he would have.

"Actually, Mrs. Swenson—Susanna," Eric told her, as brightly as he could, "you're looking very well." He aimed to go on from there to say that she might be surprised, when the hair was gone, by how interesting the face can look. Then he could have suggested removing the beret. But something—something that came from Mrs. Swenson rather than from him—prevented all of this. He remained perched on the stool, and for a long moment she studied herself in the mirror, examining her own image carefully, as if to remember it. Fronds of grey hair peeked out from under the edge of the beret.

"I lost weight," she said with a shrug. "Do you have kids yet?" Eric explained how he wasn't the settling type.

"Try not to think that way," she told him. "And don't leave it too long. It's the best thing you'll ever do. My two are busy with their own lives now, of course. I don't want to worry them. I don't tell them all the details. And I was putting this off because once I've had it done everything will be much more obvious." Her eyes settled on his face. "The thing is," she continued, "it's like there's a wall of glass between you and everyone else, even your nearest and dearest, except, of course, for people who've got it too. But they can want to get almost too close, and it's not them, somehow, that one needs."

Eric groped for words, found none, stared back at her.

"I'm sorry," he began.

"Ach—it's only *hair,*" she interrupted, suddenly looking away. "Please start."

So there it was: the once-long dark-honey hair, now in a short, greyish bob, thinning in patches. He stood behind her; their eyes met in the glass. Out of habit, Eric ran his fingers through the hair and smiled at the mirror-woman looking steadily back at him.

"I have some hats in my bag," she said. "I don't normally wear one and I didn't know what to get. I trust you'll help me choose the best one afterwards?"

He managed a nod, picked up the comb, explained how he would approach it in stages, and then made a pretense of sectioning the head. It was as if he were on stage, in a play.

He flattened some of the thin, dry stuff between his fingers and snipped off a bare two inches. The hair shed constantly, as soon as it was touched. He worked fast, looking down at the gleam of the scalp, the stray hairs, and then up into the mirror to check. The shorter hair did actually look better—less untidy, more solid, stylish almost—though also more severe.

"Go on," she said. He combed again, cut it a finger's width from the scalp, then wished he hadn't, because this way it was definitely far worse. The uneven distribution of the hair accentuated the hollows of her bone structure; it made her look like a person who had been institutionalized or abused, some street crazy. In the mirror, he saw her flinch.

"Please, get rid of it!" Her papery lids sank protectively over her eyes. He turned on the electric razor. Lightly, he pressed the crown of her head until she had lowered it enough, then he worked up from the nape, exposing the entry of the spinal cord into the skull, the curves to either side, the broad plates of bone.

Some styles involved shaving the sides only, or thin bands and patterns across the entire head, but a whole head, plain as an egg—he'd never before had a client who wanted it, though, of course, in this situation, *wanted* was not the correct word. The cleared area was a bluish white, cold looking, like some kind of stone; but at the same time, as he worked, he could feel the warmth rising from her scalp.

The shaver hummed busily as he pushed the last of the soft fuzz aside, first one side and then the other. He noticed how her skull was deep from front to back, squarish at the sides, and gently domed on top; shaved, it looked oddly larger than before. He switched off the razor, slipped it in its pouch and ran his fingertips lightly over her head, checking for anything missed. Her skin, stretched over the dome of bone, was warm and slightly oily. Where the hair had been growing more strongly or had been protected from the razor by dips in the skull were rough patches, like velvet rubbed against the grain.

Her eyes closed, her forehead pulled down, her eyebrows bunched tight. The whole face was tight. It was not what he planned, but Eric's fingers found the right place, just above the pivot of her jaw; slowly, he rotated the skin there and the tissues beneath until he felt them, and then her entire jaw, loosen. He progressed little by little, downwards along the lower ridge of the skull. He supported her forehead with his left hand and continued with the right, pressing firmly into the muscles and tendons at the top of the neck where her spinal cord entered the skull—a smooth column suddenly lost, like a train swallowed by a tunnel. He raised her head again, let her balance it, then worked slowly all over the side and top of the scalp, moving the skin infinitesimally this way, then that. She let out a sigh. He placed his hands, the fingertips just separated, on her hairline and then moved them very slowly back over the entire head. When he reached the neck, he brought them closer and then kneaded the muscles there. At the end, he cupped her head in both hands before resting them gently on her shoulders.

Looking up, he saw in the mirror his neat and familiar self, standing behind an older woman who seemed half space-alien, half baby.

"There," he said. "There, it's done now, Susanna."

Her eyes were still closed. He waited.

When Susanna saw herself, she put her hand to her mouth to catch the shriek that leaped from it. She turned to face him, breaking the mirror's spell. He wiped the moisture from under his eyes with his forefinger.

"I don't see why *you're* crying," she told him. "It *is* a shock, but I feel...not too bad. I feel better."

"Excuse me. I'm sorry!" he said, "Very sorry." There was nothing to apologize for, she said. *Please,* she said again, she did want him to help her with the hats. It would only take a minute.

Eric adjourned to the washroom. He closed his eyes and surrendered, allowed the sobs to work their way through him, amplify themselves in a room made of slate and glass. When he emerged, red-eyed, exhausted, Susanna waited calmly in front of the mirror wearing a purple knitted hat that rose to a point above her head, with plaited strings that dangled down the sides. It was like something an elf might wear.

"So?" she asked, tilting her chin, pouting a little. Exposing her bald head again, she removed the hat, offered it to him, reached into her bag and brought out an Elizabeth Taylor turban affair, purchased at a charity store, she said. She sat up straighter, raised her eyebrows.

"What do you think? Is it me?" she asked. "Or this?" She handed him the turban, pulled on a pilot's hat with earflaps, then a checkered cap.

"Susanna," he told her solemnly, but half-smiling, as he lowered the turban onto his head, "the thing is, Susanna, with good bones like yours, you can probably carry off any of these."

He sat in the back room of the salon, wearing the turban, and watched her try on the other hats. What he'd said was true. The oversized cap, the skullcap, the striped bobble hat, the felted wool helmet with a peacock feather on the side, the fine-knit toque, the white fluffy synthetic fur, the astrakhan: every one of them suited her. The first cut of the day seemed like something that had happened in a film, or a dream. He had no idea what time it was.

The Two of Us

You're a girl, though I don't know it yet. Another thing I don't know is who I am. For most of my thirty-eight-year life I did not want you; then I did, but thought it would be impossible. Now, I can scarcely believe how easy it has been, nor how much you have altered me. Breasts, belly, heart, lungs, the pigmentation of my skin, the volume of my blood—all that, of course, but this goes way beyond the physical. You have unpicked my vigilance, turned me all of a sudden into someone absent, dreamy, squeamish, alternately fierce and vulnerable. I'm even less objective than I was before. I shouldn't be giving other people advice. But that has occurred to me far too late, so here I am—along with you, of course: greased, furry, eavesdropping, hiccupping, somersaulting and thumb-sucking inside—not what I was, not quite what I will be. I am giving tutorials and running very late.

Rosemary is the last student of the afternoon. She's a short woman of perhaps sixty-five, once petite, I'd say from her hands, but now short and plump. She's wearing beige polyester slacks and a cream-coloured blouse, not tucked in. Her hair is scooped into a loose grey bun, her skin creped with age but still noticeably fine and soft. Her eyes are a clear, pale blue, but there's nothing jewel-like or penetrating about them. Like every aspect of her, they seem gentle and blurred, as if the colour has been achieved by some kind of washing and fading process over many years. She smiles, just a twitch, as she sits down beside me at the huge refectory table. Opposite is too far away; this way we have to twist to see each other but can read the text together.

"Rosemary—"

"How are you, dear?" she says at the same time. "It must be hard work this...in your condition." Her hands lie loosely, one on each thigh. She wears a thin wedding ring, no other jewellery. I'm staring too much, I think, and make myself glance away, out beyond the shade of the room at the garden, the hillside and the sky burning blue with summer's first heat. Then I come back to the room. Rosemary's two neatly typed pages are on the table between us, next to each other. Most people write reams. It's unusual to be able to see an entire piece at once like this.

"I like it," I tell her, "though it is very short. I'm not quite sure about the way you end, and that's mainly what we should talk about. Otherwise there's not much I think you need to add, or take away. It's very vivid, and clear that the child has been betrayed. And, of course, that she can't tell her aunt. You've done a good job."

"Good," Rosemary says, leaning back a little, patting a loose strand of hair back into place. "You see, I did live with my aunt. It's all true."

"Ah," I mumble, unimpressed, because *all true* tends to mean *I won't change a thing*. It makes for a more difficult and much longer session, and I'm already very tired and increasingly aware of your foot in my ribs and an ache, high up in my back, from sitting so long here at this table, necessarily further back than is comfortable for reading.

"This incident is part of a longer story," Rosemary explains. "It's not supposed to be a story on its own. So I didn't want to make it end properly because I've done other bits that come later." She smiles, then adds wistfully, "Such a strange family, we were."

At this point she waits, looking straight at me, for some kind of reply, for encouragement to continue. And if I were my proper, professional self, I would protect both of us by talking about the problems and blessings of using autobiographical material, the questions it raises, the ways it can be used as a springboard for fictional ideas. I'd be asking: What is your aim with this piece of work? How long will it be? Have you got a sense of the structure? But as it is, I run my eyes over Rosemary's face, meet the pale blue eyes (mine are similar, but newer) and let them lead me astray. I ask: "How, strange?"

I'm busy flexing my shoulders, stretching my neck, feeling you take up new positions in the spaces I've made, and I just don't think where this might lead. Though thankfully, given what she says next, I know it's not the sense of a voice you recognise, just the sound. And Rosemary's voice is as brisk and bright as waitress announcing the special of the day.

"The thing is," she tells me, "my mother's father had been through the first world war and couldn't bear the thought of another one, so he shot himself." She pauses a moment. "And then, once he was gone, my mother, poor woman, tried to kill herself too, many times, in most ways you can think of." This too feels like a pause, not an ending. And while I'm not keen on all this suicide, something, perhaps Rosemary's face (it attracts me; I'd like to touch it, to test the softness that I see against my own skin), encourages me to trust that there will be something good on the other side of it. So I wait, my attention shifting between her and you and the window. It's another new thing: these days, I find I can more easily wait.

"Then," she says, "as well as that, my mother tried to kill me and my brother. Twice, that I remember. I was six, he was four." She taps the paper between us with her forefinger, the skin pale and freckled, the nail neatly filed and polished. "That was just before this happened. It's why we had to go and live with our aunt, you see."

"Your mother tried to kill you! How? And why?" The words jump out and I wish immediately that I had not asked, because I don't want to know. In the past, I might have, but these days I have to close my eyes when blood is spilled in the cinema. I, who once wrote with relative ease of a variety of horrors (including infanticide), who invented diseases (as if there weren't already enough), find cruelty of any kind both more difficult and more painful to imagine than I used to, and cruelty to children impossible, even though I know it is real. And as for tragedy, I push it right away. I refuse to know, as if that might make it go. I want shadows banished, loose ends tied; I long for resolution. I want the world to be better, fast, so that you, the space traveller coming slowly to earth, will be safe all your long life.

"Oh," Rosemary says softly, "this is turning into some sort of confessional, which I really didn't mean." But all the same, she smiles her soft, crinkly smile and goes on with it. And my swollen heart beats harder, in case I have to do something: extricate myself, fight her, shout, run.

"I'm going backwards from the end and I haven't written this bit yet," she says. "The poor woman couldn't cope. War again, and she thought that the

German tanks were going to come rolling over the hill, so she'd better save us from them and whatever they might do. It unhinged her. The first time, she tried to gas us, along with herself, of course. We got away because she passed out first. But the very next day she cut our wrists. I climbed on top of a cupboard and managed to get out through a window to a neighbour's house, and again we were saved. My mother was hospitalized, of course, and, as I've said, we went to live with my aunt."

Rosemary calmly unbuttons the cuff of her blouse for me to see the scar, thin and white now, almost innocent in appearance.

"It's a terrible story," I say. Though, of course, it is her life. It strikes me as I speak that it is the story of a mother who could not bear the thought of tragedy and longed for resolution. "The scars are so neat," I tell her. Incredible, I think, that so much suffering can be squeezed into such small marks.

Though, actually, there's more.

"Until I had my own daughter," Rosemary says, "I didn't truly understand my mother. But after Susanna was born I was in a dreadful state. I often wanted to kill myself. These days you'd be prescribed a tablet to sort you out, but back then they didn't even have a name for depression. So I pitted myself against it. It was the idea of the suffering of others, of my little girl later in her life, that kept me from suicide. I understood my mother then. I forgave her. Maybe she was not quite so strong as I was, perhaps she had more to bear. Really, she was a gentle woman; she meant no harm. It was a perverted form of love."

This must be the end. To make certain, I name it.

"You broke the pattern," I say. "You stopped it from repeating. You made something else happen instead."

"My dear," Rosemary says, leaning back. She pulls her cuff down but leaves it unbuttoned. "My dear, I only had the one. And she is forty now, married to a lovely man. They are very happy as they are and have decided they definitely won't be having any children. Let me tell you, when Susanna told me that, I wanted to cry for relief! 'It's really over now,' I thought. 'Everyone is safe. Now everything will be all right.' I believe that. I know it will, and that's why I want to write all this down. Though somehow," she adds, "it's harder than I thought."

How dare you, I think, the flesh tightening on my arms, my stomach suddenly hard as the stretched muscles contract, practising for birth. How dare you tell me such a sad and terrible story? Your mother tried to kill you and your daughter killed her children before they even existed. What kind of ending is that?

Of course, if I were my proper, professional self, I'd be saying: isn't this a wonderful example of the way meaning is construed according to our pre-existing ideas? Doesn't it just show how everything is a matter of interpretation?

For a moment I'm too angry to say anything at all. Then I look across at Rosemary, who is smiling back at me with her clear gaze and her hands loose in her lap, and everything melts. I know for sure that she too is a gentle woman who means no harm. She is sitting next to me on the wooden bench, but, at the same time, she still lives inside the story she's told. She's in an old-fashioned kitchen that smells more every minute of gas, reaching above her head for a door handle that's just out of reach. She does get out. But the very next day it's going to happen all over again in a different way.

Rosemary gathers her papers and slips them into a file, the file into a plastic bag.

"I'm glad you liked it. And good luck with—" she gestures uncertainly at where you are, and then she's gone.

I have been no use to her at all. How ever to make a happy ending out of this?

I sit alone for a while in the shadowy room, close my eyes and wait, eyes closed, sunk down in myself so low that I can feel the slightest thing. As happens occasionally, you've fallen still, and I want you to come back. For a long time, there's nothing. Just the sounds of others in the house and garden, the smells of food being prepared, my own breath going in and out. Then, at last, a muddle of movements comes all at once, some kind of impossible gymnastics, an origami of flesh.

Elated, I stand and make my way to the stairs, climbing slowly to my room. And with each tread that is left behind, I forget Rosemary's terrible story a little more, until it has shrunk to a tiny nothing at the back of my head, to be written as "Rosemary," underlined twice, in the margin of my notebook. I'm doing it for both of us, because this is how we must go: muffled, blinkered and blind, empty of knowledge, fearless, deaf to warnings and ignorant of history. You and I, the two of us, moving on, but also going back to where everyone has been before.

There, at the very start, is no story at all, but a beginning from which everything will unfold.

The Perfect Day

It's a warm day in late May, just perfect, and I'm as hopeful about this outing as I am desperate. The two of them, them and me, the three of us, we've always squabbled. Wrangled. Fought. Over the decades there have been huge eruptions and long, siege-like silences, along with a great deal of routine sniping. Peace has occurred, but it's not been the norm. I have tried—and failed, sometimes spectacularly—to do differently. Yet none of us has ever quite given up, and here we are again, crowded this time, into my father's small room in the care home.

All three of us know that time is running out. We have two days until I fly home across the Atlantic, and I shan't see my parents again until the next visit in September. If I see them: they've reached that age. What we want is simple enough: the afternoon spent in some kind of harmony, enjoying each other's company and sharing the casual pleasures of existence. It must be possible, I tell myself, as my mother and I climb the stairs. And I yearn, as well, for something to hold onto—a memory or a talisman, proof of some kind.

Dad's small room is crammed with furniture: the bed, two large armchairs, one smaller chair, TV, side tables, bookcases, walker. Almost ninety, he only recently moved here. He needs a lot of help with practical things, forgets the day of the week, but remembers swathes of nineteenth-century verse. He has abandoned brilliantine and allows what is left of his hair—bright white and very sparse—to stick straight up, the pink scalp gleaming through. Imagine also some lopsided bifocals, slipped halfway down his nose. It's an owlish style that I somehow like, though it's disconcerting that our eyes now meet dead level, instead of me having to look up.

My mother is the same age but forgets nothing at all, still lives independently, and even rides a bicycle now and then. Once beautiful, still proud of her appearance and very well-presented, Mum has always been a fighter. She is tiny, sharp-eyed, vigorous, and fitter than many people my age. But she's never been strong on sympathy or patience and now, watching my father prepare for the drive—the slow lifting of each swollen foot, its painstaking insertion into a shoe positioned just so, the push downwards, the grind against the shoehorn, *Thank you, dear*—I can tell from the set of her jaw that she is both bored and appalled.

To rise from his high-seated chair, Dad leans forward, gripping its arms, then pushes down with his entire strength. Someone has to be waiting with the sticks, and then there's that last, precautionary visit to the toilet: pants dropped to the floor (at this point, he curses) then hauled up with the grabber and somehow fastened again. Breath hisses between his teeth. Mum grips the arms of her chair, her foot tap-tapping on the floor.

"Let me put on my own hat!" he snaps when she plonks it on his head. Still, she lets that pass, and he keeps the hat on. And he is prepared to go through with all this. He's not given up. He wants to get out and his face is rapt as we drive through the lush, tree-lined streets and on into the Cotswold Hills.

"What's that?" he asks. "Lilac? Ceanothus! This view—" he says, "I'd forgotten!"

The foliage is fresh and delicate, paler than it will soon become. Horse chestnuts thrust up, pink and white candles of bloom. May trees explode pink in all directions, like bubble-gum fireworks. Banks are rampant with cow parsley and comfrey, foxglove and buttercup. In every village the famous Cotswold stone glows gold behind gardens quivering with colour. "Marvellous," Dad says. "The journey is as good as the destination. Where did you say we're going?"

"I told you!" Mum says, "Snowshill!"

We overtake horses, pass fields of ewes and lambs and quite soon find ourselves taking the final turn into the manor grounds. According to the book, this is a five-star attraction, accessible, with a good café.

Dad struggles out of the car by pulling hard on the door while I hold it firm. Bent double, wielding the two sticks, he crunches slowly over the gravel towards the entrance.

It's when we reach the ticket desk that Mum grabs my arm, hisses: "It's a waste buying your father a ticket! He'll hardly see any of it!" I pull air into my lungs, release it slowly.

"Never mind. We've come all this way," I point out. "I'll get one anyhow."

At this, Mum scowls. "Made of money, are you?" she says, then strides away, turns her back on me and glares out of the window, and I realize, too late, that she was trying to persuade the receptionist to allow Dad in for free and that now she will be angry with me for being so dense. Nonetheless, I intend to keep smiling and move on through the kind of day I want us all to have. I purchase the tickets, my father propped on his sticks, frozen and silent, beside me.

There's a sweaty uphill hike pushing a borrowed wheelchair, then a ten-minute level stroll through more wildflowers and blossoms. The formal gardens at Snowshill are terraced down the hillside and impossible for my father to venture into. Still, the view across the valley is soft and intricate.

He studies the leaflet and reads us the high points: Derelict sixteenth-century farmhouse bought by Charles Wade in 1921. Architect and collector. Arts and Crafts movement. He reads perfectly, but very carefully, like a child who has not quite mastered the art of anticipation.

*

I heave Dad out of the wheelchair: More gravel, four steps. A metal bar at the threshold. Uneven flagstones. We step into a musty smell, dark rooms with muslin blinds and wormy beams. Another step. Dad's swollen hands clutch the two sticks. His eyes search the gloom.

What is all this stuff? Will he like it?

We examine carvings and several large, intricate model ships. The docent, a plump woman in a pleated skirt with a name tag that says "Sara" pinned to her cardigan, steps forward to tell us more about the eccentric and impassioned Mr. Wade, who had no shortage of funds and loved a well-made object of any kind. The entire house, she says, is filled with the fruits of his obsessive collecting, all of it, as he instructed in his will, unlabelled. Dad's eyes flick between Sara and a large iron chest. The curlicues of metal we see in the lid are just to protect the mechanisms, she explains, to prevent things from getting caught in the levers. It's an armada chest: an iron box with locks that shoot under a ridge on each side, making it impregnable. Half of every sailor's wage used to be saved for him, or for his widow, and stored by the Admiralty in boxes like these.

"Remarkable!" Dad pronounces. "To think they were making pension contributions back then!" He'd be appalled to know that these days his own workplace pension just about covers his care at the home.

We inch into the Dragon Room, so named because it's the kitchen, and the fireplace used to smoke. The docent here is Graham, a smiling man with iron-grey hair who announces that it's his eightieth birthday today. A display of door locks covers the wall behind him, and suits of armour stand either side of a gallery to the left.

Everything and everyone has a story. You could spend half a day in this one room, Dad points out, and there are sixteen more to explore—but he's beginning to wonder about lunch... Working against the flow of visitors, we emerge—over the metal strip, down the steps—and this time catch a buggy that runs us over to the restaurant.

Dad spreads a napkin in his lap, leans forward and begins to eat. He's never been shy of food, but his appreciation of it has grown of late, and this is a good solid meal—meat, gravy, potatoes—after which he wants to linger over coffee and dessert, whereas Mum prefers to see the rest of the house. "After all," she says, "we've paid for it." And there are sixteen more rooms to see. Less could be more, I feel.

"You'd best stay with him," she says, striding off.

*

"Look," Dad says when I bring him his cake; he gestures through the lobelia-fringed window at a young woman in a red cardigan, sitting amongst a large group at one of the outside tables. "She's cold, don't you think?" His voice is low, though no one is close by. "Look at her shoulders. And her husband next to her: that sweater goes up to his ears, but he doesn't think to offer it to her. Rather selfish. I don't like him. She could be—you know—expecting, don't you think? And that's her mother to the other side, you see? Same nose." Dad slides the fork through his chocolate cake, slips a glistening morsel into his mouth. He reaches for his coffee and looks over at me, his blue-grey eyes meeting mine over the top of his lopsided glasses, and then his gaze returns to the unknown girl in the red cardigan, and his eyes drink her up.

I'd like to leave this story now, while it is consoling. My father is close to the end of his life. These are his last years and every movement is conscious and often painful work, and yet, as we sit together in the café watching the woman in the red cardigan, there's no doubting the keenness of his pleasures or the strength of his attachment to the world. His enjoyments have been distilled. What was perhaps once diffused across his entire life creating a vague sense of well-being is now concentrated in an intense appreciation of a few good things: fresh coffee, chocolate, flowers, sports on TV and people-watching on a summer afternoon.

But it grows cooler, and by the time Mum returns, full of what she has seen—an entire floor full of antique bicycles! Incredible pottery! So many chairs!—Dad is complaining that he's cold.

"He doesn't like a breath of wind to blow on him," Mum tells me, rolling her eyes. I produce the beige sweater she chided me for bringing along on a day like this. "He'll soon warm up in the car," she says.

"What would you like?" I ask Dad.

"I'm cold," he tells us again, and removes his glasses. One each side of him, we tug the sweater over his head, feed his arms in. It's as his hands begin to emerge that things become difficult. Try as I might, I can't get my side on, though Mum succeeds.

"It's too tight!" Dad says, lifting his hand.

"You asked for it!"

"But it's too tight," he repeats. She turns to me, livid. Things—the dropped plate or missing glove, the stained carpet, the burnt pan—have always had a terrible power over her.

"That care-home laundry has shrunk a perfectly good sweater! I'll have words with them," she says. I think, but don't say, that it's just as likely that Dad's wrists, like his feet, ankles and fingers, have swollen. In any case, his left hand is definitely bigger than it was a minute ago and he sits there half in, half out while we argue.

"Leave it," Mum tells me. "He said he was cold." My father, eyes wide, says nothing, and this—his abdication at crucial moments of the struggle—has always been an issue. He's not innocent, my sister always points out. He has a role.

"What do you want, Dad?" I ask, playing mine.

"He'll say he wants it off, then he'll say he's cold again!" Mum tells me. I, who have always taken his side, ignore her.

"It hurts!" Dad says again. I begin the removal process, starting with the easy arm. When I get to Mum's side, she doesn't move.

"Excuse me," I say. Jaw clenched, she stares straight ahead, blocks my way. I crouch down, face her.

"Excuse me," I repeat. Somehow it helps to be in a public place. "Excuse me, but I am not going to make my elderly father sit in the car for an hour with the circulation to his hands cut off. If that drives you wild, you're just going to have to put up with it." Mum springs up and strides over to the ice cream cabinet. Out of the corner of my eyes, as I tug the sweater arm free, find the glasses, and help Dad up, I see her carry a choc-ice over to the desk, exclaim at the price, then return her choice to the cabinet. Silently, slowly, we three make our way back to the car.

Why are we like this? Why can't we all see how little time there is left? It seems impossible to do other than we have always done. Though after all, I console myself, today could have been far worse. I turn up the heat, start the engine and leave Snowshill behind.

Next to me, Dad is already asleep. Mum, sitting in the back, gazes out at the country for some time before she sighs, leans forward and says, loudly, right in my ear, "That, dear, was a perfect day."

Nip, tuck. Omit, forget. I should do the same, but have never had the gift. Birds dart in front of the car. Drifts of blossom carpet the road. And knowing that Mum, too, wants to improve upon our shared reality is no small thing. The May colours brighten, waver and spill over as I tell her: yes, it was.

Dear Son

THE FLAT WAS ON THE first floor of an Edwardian building. Leading up to it from the communal entrance was one straight flight of perfectly ordinary stairs, carpeted in blue, with the original turned banisters and polished mahogany handrail intact. Greg followed as his mother—even larger now than she had been at Christmastime—panted her way up, gripping the handrail tightly and pausing every four or five steps for what she called "a little rest." Not yet a third of the way up she had turned slowly around and looked at him with an expression somewhere between imploring and reproachful, as if he had invented stairs and might, therefore, have the decency to carry her up, or, at the very least, supply face fresheners and drinks at suitable intervals. Greg waited behind her, the enormous suitcase propped next to his foot. Was he supposed to catch her, should she fall? She would crush me flat, he thought, as his mother stopped and turned towards him again.

"You go ahead if you want to, Son—go on," she said, and gave him what he thought of as her fake smile: fluttering lashes and all, it was a shameless copy of the one which pitched itself across her sister Alison's pert, pretty face and had brought Alison luck, men (eventually, a husband with his own business), two homes, nice cars, five children and many grandchildren. Aunt

Alison's smile was a powerful thing, but it could not be copied and his mother's attempt to do so had always embarrassed him. In any case, it was impossible to pass her and go on ahead, though once they were in the flat, he dumped the case and strode straight to his kitchen to fill the kettle. He removed the cake he had bought for her from the fridge, closed the stainless steel door and pressed his forehead against the metal. Four days! Impossible. Why had he done this to himself?

Dear Son, his mother had written with a dark blue ballpoint on a small sheet of pale pink paper. This use of the word "Son," capitalized, this insistence on the indelible connection between them, was another thing that drove him mad. Did he not have a name? Had she forgotten it? *Dear Son,* she had written, and he could imagine her doing it, at the kitchen table, her vast, soft shoulders hunched over the tiny piece of paper. *Dear Son, It is lovely to hear from you, I was worrying. I am so glad that the police found your wallet, and the money still in it too!* Oh, he'd wanted to tear the letter in half and toss it in the bin unread. He knew exactly where it was leading, but he forced himself to read on, just in case there was something medical or legal that he needed to know or do.

What luck, when you had let it drop out of your pocket like that! I am really pleased for you. And about your friend moving into the spare room, that will be a big help to you with your mortgage, I'm sure. My news is that I went to Betty's on Saturday for her birthday, and on Wednesday to the bingo because I hadn't used my outings money on Saturday. Dave and Angie and me had a small win shared between us. I am putting it towards my holiday. I booked it last week with a fifteen percent discount, which the agent got for me. I put down £40 and I have to save the rest by August. If I don't manage it, I can't go. It is very hard to save out of what I get but I will give it a good try.

It is chilly here so I am not going out. I have made soup and will have some of that now to warm me up. I know you are busy but this is always your home too, Son, and your room is always made up. Your loving Mother.

He'd sat with the letter in his bright kitchen with the granite worktops, steel appliances, skylights and glass-fronted cabinetry cleverly lit from inside and below. It was a far cry from the old, dark, terraced house where he had grown up and from which he had bolted south at the first opportunity, to college, the big city, men, freedom, life itself. His mother had inhabited that house for over thirty years, breathing its smells of cooking and mildew, peering out from windows beaded with condensation. In his mind, it was always winter there, and the wallpaper, although it had perhaps been replaced over the years by similar prints in similar colours, was the same vague, faded floral pattern. She sat in front of the gas fire watching the vast television set, her feet up on a stool, her slack face sheened with sweat, her body open, porous, absorbing the bright colours and surges of studio laughter. Her hair was thinning a little. She had no neck at all, just folds of skin and fat. In the kitchen, the same chart from Weight Watchers had been pinned to the back of the door for as long as Greg could remember—longer.

"Oh, god, it's pathetic, it's impossible!" Greg had said to Luke when he tried to explain it all, how for twenty-three years his mother had been living on a mixture of social security payments and the tiny pension his father had left, accepting, occasionally, some small job the family network found or created for her, only to discover after a week or two that it was in some way impossible or bad for her health. It was as if, he had long thought, she was expecting to be rescued, to have someone—that was, him—bring her the life his father had, by dying, failed to provide. Upstairs in her bathroom were two ancient bottles of cheap scent that had stood there—the same bottles, their labels fading—since he was a child. And it was impossible to fill the bath properly without the water growing cold, so slowly did it seep from the furred taps. And, yes, there was mould in the grout between the tiles, a damp stain on the wall. But somehow none of these things made him want to deal with the other appeal in the letter and send his mother a cheque to pay for her holiday or to help fix the place up. This was what was expected of him, not just by his mother but also by the phalanxes of aunts, uncles and cousins who lived within driving distance of her, and were pointedly generous on special occasions. 'Your mother is helpless and hopeless,' they all seemed to agree. 'It's a burden to be carried by the rest of us, but particularly you, her nameless son.'

As if, he wanted to say, it was not enough to have been brought up by her!

Dear Son: with each year it seemed to him more ludicrous and inappropriate, more shameful, more mutually humiliating. He thanked the lord for what was left of the welfare state and shirked what everyone seemed to agree was his responsibility—until, periodically, the pressure became unbearable. Then, with bad grace, he would capitulate and send expensive flowers, some absurd gift. He had spent months in therapy about it all, getting nowhere, and now he skimmed the letter across the table, over the edge, onto the floor.

"I'm not going up there more than twice in a year! And I am not going to pay for her damn holiday!" he told Luke.

"Okay, okay," Luke grinned and got up to open a window. "It's not my fault, you know." But later, in the comfortable half-darkness of his bedroom, Greg could not sleep. Luke lay next to him, twisted across the bed like something out of Michelangelo. They were both healthy, under thirty, more or less faithful. They had been with each over for over a year. He was lucky, Greg thought, and perhaps it was this feeling of good fortune which allowed guilt about his mother to seep through as he lay there, breathing softly in and out.

He had allowed himself to consider that it might work if she visited him, instead of him travelling up there. Luke would have to go away so that she could have the room that was nominally his. He would buy her a train ticket, he'd thought, mail it to her. They could go out for dinner one night, a show the next...

And now, it was real. His mother, her face filmed with perspiration, patted the sofa next to her. He sat instead on the other one, opposite. She smiled her smile again and sipped her tea.

"Lovely," she said. "I do like it best from a pot. This is a very nice flat. Lots of room! I see you've got central heating. You must be so cosy here. You have some lovely things, Son."

"Convenient for work," he mumbled.

"That's nice," she said. There were large damp patches under the arms of her pink nylon blouse. "Delicious," she commented on the cake. "Naughty, but nice! It's good to get my breath after those stairs. I'll go to the bathroom in a minute." Please, he thought, and when she did, he called Luke's mobile.

"It's not working," he told Luke, thinking with longing of his lover's lean, self-sufficient body, his dense, curly hair. "I can't do this."

"Oh well," Luke said in a flat, sensible voice. "It's not for long, is it?"

"It took her half an hour to get up the stairs. I nearly had to ring for the fire brigade." A burst of manic laughter at the other end of the line made Greg feel immediately better.

"Well, you already know what I think," Luke said. He had made it clear, when the visit was presented to him, that he wasn't keen on disappearing for two days. He wanted everything out in the open. He'd offered to do half the talking and take half the flak. After Greg's refusal, Luke had been quiet for a couple of days. With anyone else, there would have been a row, but Luke didn't work that way; he detached himself, and later returned. Though of course, there was always the worry that one day he would not.

"I could still come home," he said now. "I'm only at the gym. But I'm catching a train to Brighton in an hour's time, and then you're on your own."

"Thanks," Greg said, "I'll stick to the plan." He heard his mother flush the toilet and then fumble with the lock on the bathroom door. "Why should she get you as well?" he added in a whisper. "And it would be a huge turnoff. You'd think I'm going out to turn out like a male version of her. Or that I already am, secretly, inside."

Luke laughed again. "Well, then," he said, still chuckling, "what time do you pick up the Lady Jayne?"

"Six," Greg said. It was only two hours.

He showed his mother to Luke's room. Lovely, she said, staring at the artistic but definitely male nude photographs on the wall. Greg retreated to his own room to have a shower in the ensuite, thinking that if he dragged it out, it would be time to go out by the time he emerged. It's not for long, he reminded himself.

"We'll collect my friend Jayne on the way," he explained as they set off. His mother had changed into a new blouse, just like the other one but pale blue, and she had applied eyeshadow that almost matched. She sat, mountainous, beside him, handbag on her lap, watching the streets unfold. He pulled into a parking bay outside a block of flats, taking care not to bump his hand into her thigh as he used the gearshift.

Anxiety seized him again as he pressed Jayne's bell. He had not had the front to ask her outright to dress properly for the role, but his hope was that she was taking the whole thing seriously, even if she had a laugh about it afterwards. He waited with his back to the car until she emerged in a cloud of musky perfume, wearing a lacy white top and a short leather skirt, no visible studs or tattoos: it could have been worse.

"Lovely to meet you, Pauline," she said, shaking his mother's hand before she climbed into the back seat.

"Tapas?" Greg said, twisting in his seat so as to see Jayne in the back. "Spanish," he explained to his mother.

"That's nice," she said. There was a pause. "You know," she added, "I don't think I've had French food since your father died."

"Oh," he said, "quite a while, then?"

"You'd prefer a French restaurant, Pauline?" Jayne's voice cut in from behind.

"I'm sure Spanish would be nice too!" His mother coloured, then twisted around to beam at Jane.

"I don't think there are any round here," Greg said. All the same, they tracked down a bistro in Clapham.

"Thank you for coming," Greg muttered in Jayne's ear as they emerged from the car, "but you needn't go over the top!"

"I'll go where I want, sweetie," she said. "No point in being nasty, is there? Relax."

The restaurant was very dark. They had a table moved to make room for his mother, and then waited for a long time before a slender, beautiful young woman in a white apron came up to light the candle on their table.

"Voilà," she said.

"Some wine, please," Greg said. "Bottle of—"

"Pauline?" prompted Jayne.

"Well, I do like a sweet white wine," his mother said. "But don't mind me. This is so lovely. I'm having such a time! I never go out, you know."

"Sweet white," Jayne told the waitress.

"Cheers!" his mother said as it was poured.

"To your trip," Jayne added.

Greg winced at the sweetness, but they all drank deeply, and then Jayne translated the menu, every item, painstakingly. His mother ordered onion soup and a chicken dish, he and Jayne mussels, then steak and cassoulet, respectively.

He looked at his watch. Only seven! No wonder the place was deserted. He felt absolutely hollow, empty of words, and listened gratefully to Jayne's enquiries as to the details of his mother's journey, her impressions of the city so far.

The first course arrived. Dabbing frequently at her lips with a napkin his mother exclaimed, "Delicious," then fell silent. She drank her soup steadily, with concentration, resting only occasionally for a nibble of generously buttered bread. Her eyes were steady and serious. It was like some kind of communion. Greg noticed her fingers, how small they were, really, beneath the fleshy padding that had now covered even her furthest extremities, how neatly and efficiently they worked at putting the meal away. Watching her, it struck him that he had inherited his mother's enthusiasm for food, though of course he liked to think he had better taste in it than she did. He did at least alternate periods of gluttony with strict diets, and he spent long hours in the gym. Jayne too ate heartily, but only when presented with the opportunity, as now; between these times she was often distracted by alcohol, drugs, conversation, politics, dancing, the dramas of sex and romance.

"You've lived on your own ever since Greg's dad died?" Jayne asked Pauline.

"Yes, dear, that's right," Pauline patted her lips again. "He went very suddenly and it was a big shock, but at least we two had each other, didn't we, Son?" Greg tossed a mussel shell onto his side plate.

"To tell the truth," he said, "I can't remember it. Or him, and I wish you wouldn't call me 'Son' like that."

And why couldn't he remember it? That was a question he'd asked the psychotherapist many times. Why were the early years missing? Most people had memories of when they were five or six. Four, even. Had something happened, or was it just so utterly, mind-numbingly boring that he had blotted it out, emerging, already enraged, at the age of ten? He'd never know. Glaring at Pauline, he picked up his glass, drained it, filled it again.

"Gregory was such a comfort," his mother told Jayne. "A sweet boy." Smiling, she began to ease herself out of the spindly chair she was perched on. "I must visit the ladies' room."

"Oh my," Jayne said, as Greg split the rest of the wine between their glasses and ordered another bottle, dry this time. "Pretty sad."

"Don't encourage her," Greg said.

"I thought that was what I was here for," she said. "Why don't you just sit there, get drunk and let me get on with it?"

When his mother returned, her face was wet and there were splashes of water on her blouse. The table shook as she grabbed hold of it to ease her way down.

"Better?" Jayne asked.

"Oh, yes, dear. It's nice in there, lovely and cool."

More food came, islands of it on huge white plates.

"Greg takes after his father," Greg's mother said. "Even more now he's grown up. They've got the same lovely thick hair, though you can't really see that, not with it so short now." She sighed, brightened, changed tack: "The family have always been very good to me."

"That's nice," Jayne said.

"Yes," Pauline replied, her mouth full. "Alison and Bill, especially, and Hal too, and Bibs." Greg plucked up a couple of fries and drank, not knowing whether to laugh, cry or applaud.

"It's a long way for them to come, to pick me up. I don't drive."

It was with difficulty that Greg stifled the urge to jump to his feet, shouting, "Why the hell didn't you learn? I'd have paid for that, for god's sake!" He felt the room lurch slightly.

"Thank you, dear," his mother said as he filled the glasses. She set her knife and fork together on an empty plate. The waitress appeared again.

"I'd better not..." his mother said, but then Jayne leaned over and touched her gently on the arm—"Oh go on, you're on holiday, aren't you?"—and so she ordered crème brûlée.

"Shan't be a moment," Jane announced, standing. "Be good, you two." Greg imagined her in the washroom, screaming to let off steam, or else making absurd faces at the mirror. But there was no time to appreciate the image because now his mother turned her attention, for the first time in a while, back to him.

"She's a very kind girl," she told him. "You could do far worse. Where did you meet her?"

"In a club."

"I think you're very well suited," she said. What? he thought. What have you ever known about me and what I'm like or not like, what might possibly suit me? "I hope you will be very happy together." His mother's hand settled over his on the table. The contact was unbearable.

"No!" he said, pulling free. "Jayne's just a friend of mine." He wanted to vaporize himself out of the room, but he had begun and could not stop. "It's just not like that," he continued, articulating the words carefully to avoid a slur, not quite succeeding, saying, finally, "she's just a friend. I like men," he said, very loudly, to make sure it got through. "I'm gay. Bent. Queer. I've got a boyfriend."

"Oh," his mother said, as coffees and her dessert arrived.

"I was just explaining to my mother about my sexual orientation," he said, glaring at Jayne as she slipped back into her chair.

"Really?" Jayne replied, as Pauline slowly brought to her lips her first spoonful of the crème brûlée, topped with a smidge of whipped cream and a single redcurrant. "Why now? Why did we have to go through this charade first?" Greg tipped the empty wine bottle over his empty glass and looked into it to avoid Jayne's gaze.

"You two had better get a cab home," Jayne said, lighting a cigarette. "I'm going on to a party when I've finished this. I'll walk."

It was dusk, the roads heavy with summer traffic. Greg and his mother sat in silence at opposite ends of the seat at the back of the minicab that Jayne had called for them. The radio broadcast a phone-in where people called a doctor in the studio for a diagnosis of their symptoms: shortness of breath, weight loss, headaches, sore legs, itchy rash, memory lapses, and so on. The doctor, young, male, made small listening noises as the problems were outlined, asked a few questions, then, in each case, gave out some sympathy and a range of possible causes, concluding always with an strong recommendation for the caller to take themselves to their own GP.

Outside the flat, Greg fumbled for his wallet while the speakers blurted out the voice of a woman describing how it hurt her husband to urinate.

"Thanks," Greg told the driver, waving away change. He opened the door and watched his mother heave herself out, gripping the roof of the vehicle with one hand and pushing up from the seat with the other. Breathing hard, she took his arm to steady herself.

"Right," Greg said. She didn't let go of his arm, or start walking. He felt drunker than he could remember feeling before. The streetlights pulsated in time with the pulse that beat in his neck and temples. There was a scent of jasmine coming from someone's front garden or window box.

"Let's get in," he suggested. She started walking, very slowly, but still didn't let go of his arm. In this way they went up the path to the front door with its brass letterbox and number plate.

"That programme on the radio," she said as he fished in his pocket for the keys. "Is it on every night? We don't have anything like that at home." Now he was struggling to get the key in the lock. At last it slipped in and the door opened, banging against the inside wall. On the way to finding the light switch, the keys skidded out of his hand.

"What is your boyfriend's name?" she asked.

"Luke," he told her. He freed his arm and cautiously lowered himself to retrieve the keys. His head pounded; standing up made the world lurch back and forth. "Right, let's go," he said, and to steady himself, he took his mother's arm again, grasped the rail with his free hand. He looked up then and saw the stairs, brightly lit at the bottom, vanishing into blue-grey gloom half-way up and, in his drunkenness, foreshortened, twice as steep-looking as they really were.

Different Lips

JESSICA, RIGHT AT THE FRONT of the upper deck of the bus, gazed out past the ghost of her face in the window. She registered the dusty, sun-scoured streets, the Saturday shoppers—their stuffed bags, their trailing children—but most of her was taken up with remembering Simon. She was thinking especially about his lips, so very small in his face, the upper almost non-existent, the lower tiny, but plump and very pink. She was remembering how those lips met with a pucker, like a navel in the face, and were neither manly nor conventionally attractive. Yet this was precisely why she had liked them so much: few others would have the imagination to try them, to realize how very soft, yet also somehow resilient, they were and how, although they seemed narrow at first, there was always a shock of pleasure when his mouth opened up to her, wet and alive. And after this came another surprise: that such a tongue-tied and nervous man could be, in the flesh, so articulate.

She wore the pink linen dress and matching sandals she had bought with the last of her money. Her hands lay loosely in her lap. Her face showed no sign of the memories that preoccupied her. On the contrary, it had the appearance of a contemplative's face or a saint's: pale, oval, unlined, symmetrical. Behind the sunglasses, her eyes were large, slightly hooded and set wide apart beneath gently arched brows. Her nose was straight, and below it her lips were wide but not particularly plump. The impression was solemn and wise.

She had been told countless times by social workers, teachers, foster parents and even the occasional Justice of the Peace that without her looks, she would be in worse trouble than she was. Jessica had never minded trouble, but they unfailingly gave her the benefit of the doubt.

As a child, playing to the mirror, she'd wrinkle her nose, expose the rims of her eyes, turn her lips inside out to display the ridges of arteries shiny with saliva. As a woman, she had tried makeup, piercings, dirt, bad-girl haircuts—but somehow the wise, saintly mask shone through them all, pretending, it seemed to her, to know things she did not. Now, she avoided confronting it. There were other things she avoided also, and avoidance was, at least in part, why she was taking the bus that Saturday to visit Simon Stone, thinking that soon she would kiss those lips again, that it was almost certain.

The spark between them had lost some of its intensity by the time they parted, but would be easy to revive. They would hold each other and kiss—as she considered this, the inside of her own mouth flooded itself and her own neatly formed lips grew imperceptibly plumper. She imagined how kisses would lead to the undoing of a belt buckle, to the warm, velvety skin around the hard flesh of his cock. She wanted to have him for a long time, slowly, different ways. And afterwards, they would very likely go out for the friendly drink he had frequently suggested in the unreciprocated birthday and Christmas cards he had sent her over the years since they broke up. Though maybe she'd just leave, because when they were seeing each other she had often been bored with the talking side of things. Simon's voice—hesitant, high, but also loud—could be irritating. He repeated himself; he clung obstinately to his point. It would be better, under the present circumstances, to carry the good feeling straight back to the studio.

The bus lurched to another standstill, and Jessica peeled herself out of her seat, adjusted the pink linen dress and took the stairs down and out into the noise of the main road. Each step she took increased her desire until it bordered on a kind of misery. You'd better be there, she thought as she turned onto the neat, tree-lined street. The district, bordering on Notting Hill, was far better than where he had lived before. The buildings were spacious and Georgian, painted white and cream. There was a gate, a tiled path, a flight of four steps to a rather grand columned porch. There were wide double doors ranked with many bells. She stood with the sun on her back, searching for his name.

The doors unlocked with a click. It was cool inside. And there in the dimness of the first-floor landing was Simon: a tall, slightly lopsided figure.

"Jess!" he called out, gesturing for her to follow him through an unlit hall and into a large room at the front of the building. The room was shaded by venetian blinds. A fan whirred in the corner, turning slowly from side to side. A new drawing board, a stool and office paraphernalia were arranged by the far wall, a low glass table and piles of cushions in the bay window. On the table stood two glasses and a bottle of water, beaded from the fridge.

Seated, she looked at him properly for the first time. She judged his hair to be ever-so-slightly thinner on the crown of his head and cut shorter. She recognized his long-fingered hands with their baby-pink, neatly filed nails. But the lips she had crossed the city for, changing buses three times—those weren't here. Instead, a different pair lips stood out on Simon's face, fissured, bloody, and swollen to almost twice their usual size. Skin blistered from them in bubbles and rags, as if they were being barbecued.

He raised his hand towards them, stopped halfway.

"Allergy," he told her. "Stress, pollution, take your pick. I'm keeping in for a while, to see if that helps. So"—a staccato laugh—"it was lucky you called."

Lucky? What am I going to do now? Jessica thought, heavy with disappointment. She called to mind the studio, empty, waiting. She should go straight back there but it felt far too hard; she needed something to lift her up beforehand. She found his gaze and held it. His eyes, brown, liquid, hadn't changed at all, but they were no use to her.

"It must be, what, two years now?" he was saying. "So, what are you up to? Still with that production company?" Jessica nodded, swallowed. There had been difficulties with the new boss and she'd ended up moving on to a smaller, less prestigious company. After a few more months, the new place had decided not to renew her contract. She couldn't find anything else and had refused to temp, so it was a matter of going freelance, which had meant moving to a rundown studio flat in Streatham. Freelancing didn't work out, and then the bank cancelled her credit card, so she couldn't even jump on an airplane and get away from it all for a few months, which for a long time had been in the back of her mind as a failsafe. Thailand, Mexico, India—somewhere cheap. But she sat still on the cushion and didn't explain any of this to Simon, nor did she tell him about the row she'd had two weeks ago with her longest-standing girl friend, Anna, concerning the dog Jessica had adopted from the Dogs' Home to keep her company when she started to freelance.

She'd liked the dog at first, but he just stared at her all day and made her feel even more down than she had been before: not the idea. She returned him a fortnight later.

"You can't just take a dog back, like a library book," Anna had said.

"He had a holiday," Jessica joked. "Or say I fostered him."

A dog was for life, Anna said.

"Anna, nothing is for life, let alone a dog."

"I do make allowances for your background," Anna told Jessica, "but there are limits."

"Did I ever ask you to?" Jessica replied, and at the time she felt as if she had won, but Anna hadn't answered her messages since.

It wasn't just about the dog. Nothing had worked out recently. For over a year, things had been going bad. It felt as if the absurd, fall-on-your-feet luck she had taken for granted until now had just run right out and that was it. Finite. Gone. But she certainly wasn't going to explain any of that to Simon Stone, and when he asked, "Why now, Jessica?" she shrugged and looked at him and hated his lips.

"Jessica," he chided her, "you must have wanted something!"

"I was coming over this way," she insisted, sitting straight-backed on her cushion.

"I thought," he said, "maybe she's feeling down? The world's not going her way, or someone's moved out of her life, so she wants to touch an old base? To be honest,

I thought you might want, well—" He reached for the water bottle and it gasped faintly as he unscrewed its cap, and suddenly the room was full of other small sounds too: the fax machine behind him hummed and flicked a message through, a blind tapped against the window frame, bubbles in the two glasses fizzled, expired with tiny sighs.

She took her water, drank.

"You know, there's not been anyone else," he said.

No one? In the years since she'd seen him last, more people than she could think of had been all over and inside of her. There had been lips and hair, sweat, semen, hands grasping and stroking flesh, sucking, licking, biting. She couldn't imagine the loneliness of being without all that.

Stand up and walk out of here, she advised herself. Things could only get worse. But it was Simon who rose. He came around to her side of the table, settled himself next to her.

"You still look great," he told her. "Like a delinquent nun." He took her hand and her insides lurched; she pulled it away and he let go.

"Is it these lips?" he asked. "Do they bother you? We don't have to kiss. Can't, in fact." Again, his laugh set her teeth on edge. "They really hurt." He moved closer, leaned into her so that she lost her balance and found herself semi-prone in a drift of cushions.

"No, Simon," she told him.

"Why not?" he said, his hand on her breast. A moment later his other hand slid up her thigh, inside the burgundy lace underpants she'd bought at the same time as the dress; he felt her where she was still wet. A moment later he was on top of her—she could feel his heart race frantically, just as it used to, and his raw lips were inches away from her face, blood and scab in the cracks. She wrenched her head sideways.

"No!" she said again, but his hand was busy and she was half-responding, despite herself. Then he was inside her and she, Jessica, lay flat on her back, legs apart, while Simon Stone (of all people) took his pleasure from her, apparently indifferent as to her consent. But her hips were cooperating with his movements. She stopped them and then they started again. Nothing like this had happened to her before. It was almost funny, but then again, it was really not.

"There," he muttered, "there, there, there."

He made it last but finally pressed his face into the side of Jessica's neck, groaned, fell still. An answering quake passed through Jessica's body but she willed her mouth shut tight.

"Get off me!" she told him. "Simon, it's bloody well time you found someone else." He laughed, moved away to lie on his back among his cushions, post-coitally expansive.

"Don't worry," he told her. "I'm not fixated. It's just always been so easy with you because—well, because of how you are." His face broke into a grin. "Thanks."

"It wasn't what I wanted," she said pulling away. Though it so nearly was.

"You could have fooled me." Simon closed his eyes as if to sleep, and she went and cleaned herself up in his bathroom, then left. The door was on a closer and would not slam.

The homebound bus jerked forward in rough spurts, interspersed with long, throbbing pauses. Jessica, sitting in the exact same seat on the top of the bus, added what had occurred in Simon's flat to the list of things she would not think about. She focused her attention on the shoppers below, who seemed even more burdened and fretful than before. There were more of them, too—that last desperate surge before closing time. Street markets were winding down, cash machines emptying. Litter flooded the street. She noticed, tied to a railing outside Marks and Spencer, a short-haired dog with floppy ears and she was sure, absolutely sure, that it was her dog, the one she had sent back. It sat obediently but at the same time strained towards the automatic doors at the shop's entrance, every fibre of its body yearning for the person who had left it there. Who? Jessica twisted in her seat to keep the dog in sight, but the bus pulled away before anyone came out. Would Simon still send her cards? It seemed, all of a sudden, a very important thing. Nothing made sense—and that had not mattered before, but now it did.

The studio was empty. She had spent the last two weeks disposing of everything, from the futon to the computer and the TV. Laptop, phone, her collections of books, all the old CDs and shoes—all gone. She had sold what she could for whatever she could get, and then she had bought the dress and the shoes from Browns with the last of the cash: £350. *That's a good dress*, the saleswoman had said. Wearing it, Jessica walked into the windowless, damp-smelling bathroom, which automatically filled with the clatter of the extractor fan when she shut the door. She set the bath running. There was a tremor in her hands as she fumbled with the catch of the cabinet above the basin and felt along the upper shelf for the packet of razor blades. She slid one out, unwrapped it.

Then, holding it tight between forefinger and thumb, she glanced up into the mirror on the cabinet door. There was a moment during which she might have shifted her attention back to the running bath or to the blade. But it passed. She leaned forward, steadied herself by pressing the heels of both hands hard into the cool porcelain of the basin, and looked.

She saw the high forehead and even higher hairline, the wide jaw, the straight nose that held them together and apart at the same time. She weighed her eyebrows against each other, saw how the curve of the left was ever so slightly fuller than the right, and how that was balanced perfectly by the slight upward pull of her lips on the opposite side. She noted two very faint lines running parallel across her forehead, and others even fainter at the outer corners of grey-green eyes sunk in roomy sockets, and observed the delicacy of the ruffled skin on her lids. Finally, she met the eyes themselves and allowed them, their pupils wide with fear, to look back at her.

With a tiny clatter, the razor blade fell from between her finger and thumb and skittered itself still. And now there was no choice, Jessica understood, but to grow to fit this thing she had been born with, the unwanted gift from one or the other of her parents (or both: she'd never know). *A terrible process*, her smug saint's face seemed to advise her, its eyes glistening darkly with foreknowledge, with wisdom that had not been easily earned. It was too much. She strode out of the bathroom forgetting to turn off the bath water and left the empty flat, clattering down the dusty communal staircase and out into the street.

The four-lane road running alongside the park was solid with traffic. She set off uphill towards the bus stop where the payphone booths were. Her heart beat hard as she waited her turn.

The cheap restaurants and pubs nearby were filling up. People spilled out onto improvised terraces, or else just leaned on walls, glasses in hand. A few parents pushed slack-faced, sleeping children homewards, the older siblings, occupied with brightly coloured drinks and ice creams, trailing behind.

Fingering the two coins in her pocket, she closed her eyes a moment and saw Simon's face, his spoiled lips. Suppose he doesn't answer? she thought. What then?

Half a mile way in her abandoned flat, water gushed from the tap she had forgotten to close. In the phone booth, a punky boy in a studded jacket fed another coin into the slot.

Sweet Agony

THE SUN'S RAYS, GOLDEN, infrared, ultraviolet, make the world. They pour onto Livia's back, neck, and thighs, onto the soles of her feet, the peach down on her arms; they summon the blood to her skin, squeeze sweat from her pores, relax the muscles beneath. Okay, the sun can give you cancer, but it's good, too: she's making vitamin D and melatonin, she can feel the fizz of all that weird chemistry happening just beneath her skin. The towel she lies on is rough and damp, and the murky smell of the lake seeps from between the wooden slats of the dock, which rocks and creaks as swimmers climb on and dive off, the thick green water breaking into golden streaks and swirls with each dive, then resealing itself, perfect each time.

She's come to the lake every summer of her life so far: at first, she swam inside her swimming mother's womb, one small body of water suspended in a huge one, and then she was dragged over to the dock in a blow-up boat, many times, until finally she dared to splash and gasp her way over herself, terrified, that first time, of the deep, of death itself. Later, she passed afternoons with the daredevils, practised backflips, diving deep to retrieve ancient sunglasses and lost watches from the mud, or gulping air then swimming under the dock from one side to the other. Now she just basks, waiting for Tal to arrive, his mocha skin beaded silver from the swim. She thinks of his lips pressing against hers, still closed—the ache of it. The way they each know just how much the other can bear.

Suppose she says to him, Let's go back to my house. My brother is at a friend's house, my father is at work, my mother five thousand miles away. They will know not to kiss again, but instead stand and dive, swim to shore, then walk, holding hands, up the lane and into the cool, empty house. In her bedroom, with the wardrobe doors flung open and the books piled on the floor, her makeup scattered, lids strewn over her desk, she will be inside and beside and astounded by herself. He'll try to remember the things he knows he should do, the condom in his wallet. They will mess things up, not care, laugh. He'll call out her name, Liv, Liv, Liv, in the empty house. She will make him promise not to tell, though everyone at school and her mother, when she returns, will know just from the way they look at each other across the room.

His shadow briefly caresses her back and then Tal's hand is cool on her shoulder, and she sits up to face him, their cheeks brushing very close to the lips. Tugging against the force that draws them together, they pull apart, study each other. Brown eyes, blue-grey; two pairs of full lips, planes and angles of cheeks, nose, forehead. The pallor of her throat, the freckles on her nose, the shadow deepening beneath the skin of his jaw. The short, close-cut wool on his head, shaved through in stripes on one side. His hand shakes when he reaches out to tuck a strand of her hair behind her ear and they both smile—though in a way it is a terrible predicament, to know what is bound to happen, but at the same time not know: how, or when, or really—despite everything they know and imagine already—what it would be like to surrender to each other and whatever is inside themselves, and all that might or might not come of doing so, on a summer afternoon, after the lake.

The Right Thing to Say

BENEATH A FIERCE SEPTEMBER sky, the city squats in the ochre plain: a cluster of rectangular towers surrounded by a vast, ever-growing sprawl of homes. Don is driving Marla's car, the Corolla, which he cleaned out yesterday and filled with gas, to save them having to think about it today. He slows to fifty as he passes Safeway. There's no traffic; they're on 16th now.

"Nearly there," he says, patting her leg, and she nods.

"Music, love?" he asks, and this time she shakes her head. She's sitting there looking straight ahead as they sail past dusty-looking motels, a gas station, the ski rental. She wears sunglasses. Her hands are folded in her lap. No sign of the baby yet, of course. A stranger wouldn't know what she's going through. Usually she's the one who knows what to say, who wants everything put into words, but now she's fallen silent, and really, Don thinks, there probably is nothing that they haven't talked over twenty or two hundred times already. Soon they will have an answer: it just better be the one they want, okay, whoever-you-are-up-there?

There's a fifty-fifty chance. Whichever way you peer at it, it's the same. Quite big. Not small. If you had a fifty-fifty chance of winning the lottery, you'd be pretty much on the edge of your seat. It's kind of the opposite of that, multiplied.

This morning Marla dressed to make a show of strength: denim skirt, fitted, lace-trimmed blouse, jewellery—all new things he hasn't seen before. Makeup too. Don went the other way: jeans, tee-shirt.

He'd like to be able to say something, to find the right words. But his mind is full of dumb, trivial thoughts. Such as: it's a holiday, and also it's lunchtime. He and Marla could be grilling some chicken on the barbecue. What was in that marinade they used last time? He glances across at Marla again and almost asks, but stops himself.

They should be hiking Powderface Ridge or gliding along the Kananaskis in their kayaks. But instead, because Dr. Ludvigssen has decided to go on vacation tomorrow, when every other person is returning from theirs), they're going for results.

"I can't wait another month," she said. Her call.

Don waits for three Lycra-clad cyclists to waver across the crosswalk, going to the park.

After this, he thinks, he'll definitely sign up at the gym. Not that Marla has ever complained, and he is probably fitter than he looks, given his work. It's just something is needed to pull it all together.

Crushed juniper berries, he remembers. Honey. Oil. Red wine. We could make it again tonight.

The hospital blocks come into sight on the right-hand side. It's a huge place. Every kind of specialist you could ever not want to have to see.

"Do you have a gut feeling for what your result will be?" Dr. MacLeod, the psychiatrist, asked weeks ago in one of the early consultations.

"Yes," Marla said. "It's silly, I know, but I don't want to say it."

"Me?" Don said, "Yes. Marla is fine. She has to be. That's what I feel."

"The trouble with gut feelings," Dr. MacLeod said in that voice of his, subdued but insistent, "is that they have absolutely no bearing on the facts. Studies have shown that people are wrong as often as they are right. Suppose your gut feeling was wrong? I'm just asking you both to consider that, in the intervening time."

I am not wrong, Don thought.

But now, with Marla sitting stately and silent beside him as he drives towards the answer that has always been in her body, written, as the genetic counsellor explained it, in the paired genes of chromosome number four, his hands begin to sweat against the wheel.

Because they don't need to do this! They could leave the answer in its sealed envelope, turn right around, and drive back towards the mountains—go home, eat, make love, soak together in the tub, doze, dream, continue from tomorrow as before. The baby's risk is only half of Marla's. Just twenty-five per cent. They don't have to find anything out. They can just keep their fingers crossed, live for the moment, the way they have so far. Why mess—

"Lights!" Marla yells, and he jams his foot down, and the seatbelts lock, biting into their shoulders. Their heads thud into the headrests. Then there is a blissful moment of nothing at all, followed by the blare of a horn. He's way over the line and in the wrong lane too.

"Are you okay?"

"I think so," she says. "You?"

"Sorry, sorry," he says, pulling air into his lungs. Everything is suddenly brighter than it used to be. "It wasn't the idea to total us on the way! Or give us double heart attacks. Mind you, this spot would be convenient for emergency."

"True." Her lips twitch. "It's green, now."

He indicates, checks, double-checks, and cautiously takes the right, then the next right. The hospital complex, oddly still, swallows them up. Parkade six is almost empty, and he slides the car into a slot right in front of the entrance, then leans back in his seat and turns to look at her.

"We're ten minutes early," he says.

"Maybe they'll see us anyhow. We might as well go in. I can use the washroom."

But I don't want to go in, he thinks, not until we have to.

She takes her sunglasses off and kisses him on the lips, her mouth hot, tasting of mint.

Maybe, he thinks, she'll change her mind about this, even now.

But of course she climbs out of the car and he follows her. Again, he badly wants to say something. The right thing. Not just "I love you." Something more like: I'm with you. And if it's bad news—

Bad news? It won't be. No way.

"Marla—" is what he manages as the entrance doors slide open. He follows her into the elevator, out again.

The place is deserted, all the grey chairs empty, no receptionist, no bustle of file-wielding people passing through. No sick people either, and that, he thinks, is a relief. He glances at his watch. It's ten past one.

"They'll be here soon," she says. "I won't be long." He watches her until she turns the corner, then eases into one of the chairs and finds himself facing the leaflet rack, where, he knows, innocent-looking booklets and concertina-folded sheets of paper harbour phrases such as: "This is a late-onset, inherited brain disorder that causes progressive deterioration of the physical, cognitive and emotional self." He digs his fingers into his palms and squeezes his eyes shut.

*

Marla lets the water run, just for the sound of it, the way it rushes on. Makes an effort to breathe slowly. Continues with the mantra she has made for herself: Even if I have the gene, it could be ten years before there are any signs at all. So I can keep on how I am, or I can do something different, if that's what I want. Even if I've got the gene, it doesn't follow that it'll go for me the exact same way that it went for Mum. It might just be physical, just the movements, rather than mental. To start with, at least. I'm fine right now. Even if I have the gene, we could still have the baby, perhaps. So long as. Please.

Nothing's different, she thinks, daring the face in the mirror to argue, except I'm choosing to know. Knowledge makes no difference to the facts, but it might make a difference to what I do.

What Don does. We do.

She shuts off the tap, meets her own gaze in the mirror and decides against touching up her lipstick.

Well, she thinks, this is no good. These are the last few minutes of not knowing and I'm spending them in a toilet! There should be a special suite of rooms for this, an atrium with ferns and vines and a lily pond, classical music softly playing from speakers you can't see. Or the singing of birds.

It will be all right, Marla tells herself.

*

At the wedding, Don remembers, it was very clear. They stood next to each other in the shade, facing the guests, and repeated their vows after the registrar. There was a script. They took turns. He felt her beside him, the body he knew so well cased in its strange, elaborate dress. His voice came out loud and clear, and despite the preceding weeks of jokes with friends about "needing to be committed," he felt absolutely sure. He promised there would be no others. He promised to be with Marla in sickness or in health, and certainly he thought he knew what he was promising, because she had told him about it on their third date, and at the beginning, he had been with her to visit her mother one Christmas. He had seen how she was.

They were married in July, on Ed Wagner's ranch. All the fields were baled, and beyond them you could see the mountains rearing up, purple-grey, and some clouds boiling yet further above.

Her father said they deserved the best of everything in life and raised a glass. His father made a rambling speech about Marla's brains and Don's hands and how at least they'd always have a roof over their head and a table to eat at and never be short of conversation, and she cupped a hand to his ear and whispered that hands were all very well but there were other things he had about him too—and guests who saw the whisper somehow guessed what she was saying, banged on the table and roared.

But here's the thing: despite everything she said, despite the recent assault course of leaflets, video, psychiatrist, counsellor, neurologist, despite all their best efforts and his own, despite thinking he had taken it on, he has never really been able to imagine that someone might actually say to Marla, "You have it, too." He's listened, he's looked, but he has never believed it, not even for a moment until now, here in the Foothills Hospital's deserted waiting room, where he sits in a kind of vertigo, driving his nails into his palms and asking himself: What if there is bad news? How will I be for her? What will I do, what will I say to her as she turns to me?

And then, as it sinks in, what will he find himself feeling? When you say "I do," even to sickness and health, you're not thinking exactly of this. Will he know the right things to do, and be able to do them? Be able to bear it, to change himself into what is needed? Or will he run, as Marla's father did (and no one, not even Marla, really blamed the man)?

At work, he gets the instructions or drawings, sees what's required in his mind's eye. He lines up the materials and tools, begins where it has to be begun, and works his way through. Measure twice, cut once. Study the grain. So long as your attention is on the job, it will work out. But this is not the same, and he doesn't know.

And now it's 1:15, and a tall woman in loose, elegant clothes is walking towards him.

"Don. I'm Juliette." He remembers her from the first appointment. Warm hands, soft voice, a way of being able to look you in the eye without staring. He likes her.

"She's in the washroom," he says, just as Marla appears. He notices his heart beat harder as she stands close to him and reaches for his hand.

"Here we are, then," Juliette says. "Dr. Ludvigssen is here too, so we can go right ahead now, but of course, as I said, if you're having any kind of misgivings, we can put a hold on this."

"I want to go ahead," Marla says.

Juliette nods, waits a moment. "I'll call Dr. Ludvigssen and tell her we're on our way." As she walks to reception and picks up the phone, they turn into each other and embrace, their hands gripping hard, squeezing themselves against each other, their minds emptied out.

"This way," Juliette says, and Marla follows, then Don. A left, a right, two lefts, right again.

When they came before, it was full of people, even in the corridors. Now, there's just a faint rustle of clothes, their own muffled footsteps, the building's permanent hum. Names on the doors with strings of letters after them. FRCPC. FCCMG.

"With your permission," Juliette says, "I'll come in with you. In case I'm needed."

The door marked "Dr. Ludvigssen" is half open. There's a desk, two chairs in front of it, one beneath the window, and an examining couch on the wall opposite the desk. A pink-cheeked woman with a shock of almost-white hair is standing behind her desk. She greets Juliette, who goes to stand by the window, clasps Marla's and Don's hands, waves them into their chairs, and sits down as they do so. How was their journey over?

Come on! Don thinks, as Marla explains that the drive was a little tense. Hurry! he orders the doctor in his head.

"I won't keep you waiting. I have your lab report here, Marla," Dr. Ludvigssen says, and there's just not enough space in the room. Not enough air, either, Don thinks. Marla's hand in his is damp, hot. And now, suddenly, it's going too fast: the doctor slips her paperknife into the corner of the envelope and draws it across, sawing through the fibres. She replaces the knife in her desk drawer, extracts and unfolds the letter, flattens it on the desk and leans over it. Marla closes her eyes. Don, though, watches the doctor scan the page. Her face is very still, mask-like, and there's a kind of high-pitched ringing in his ears, a feeling of imminent explosion in his chest, and then, the moment before she speaks, he sees the corners of her eyes and mouth relax.

"It's good news," she says.

Don jumps to his feet and yells, "Marla!" and when she looks up at him, her face is as he has never seen it before: eyes startled wide, her mouth a perfect *O*.

Then she turns back to Dr. Ludvigssen.

"Are you sure?" she asks.

"Yes. Completely. Your results are well within the normal range." Don pulls his chair right up and sits again with his arm tight around Marla's shoulders as Dr. Ludvigssen continues, nodding, smiling, speaking slowly. When she uses the word "unambiguous," she corrects herself and says "completely clear." She shows them the report from the lab. Her finger points to numbers and abbreviations, to a line of waveforms wiggling across the page, pretty much incomprehensible to a finishing carpenter, or even a school teacher, except that it means that everything is all right. The disastrous piece of code has not been handed down, and that is the end of it.

Marla wipes her eyes and leans back in her chair. One of her arms is flung out to the side. It's as if all tension has been sucked from her body.

"Thank you," she says.

"I'm very pleased for you." Dr Ludvigssen glances at her colleague standing forgotten by the window and then continues, her voice very gentle: "But, you know, we can't take the credit there. Good or bad, we don't make these results, nor does the lab. We just bring the news. Good or bad, as I say."

"Thank you both," Marla insists. "Thank you for coming in today." And now Juliette is explaining that even when they have fantastic news like this, people do sometimes have unexpected reactions, and to get in touch if they need anything or have any questions. Otherwise, she will call in a month or so. She stands, and the doctor follows suit.

"Why not stay in the office awhile?" Juliette suggests. "It's really not a good idea to drive straight away. Take a few minutes, and leave when you're ready."

"Enjoy your holiday!" Don tells Dr. Ludvigssen, and as he pumps her hand up and down, he notices the dampness on her cheeks.

How often, he thinks, do those two have to do this?

They are alone. A breath of outside air pushes at the blind, shifting the light and making a faint clattering noise. The room and everything in it—the poster about neurons above the examining table, the blue mug on the bookshelf, the film of dust on the blinds, the dead plant on Dr. Ludvigssen's desk—all of it seems alert, almost alive. Even the air is different, charged and delicious. They breathe deeply, filling themselves up. They turn their chairs to so that they can absorb each other with their eyes.

I want to remember this, Marla thinks. I want to remember it all: Don looking back at me, the way the room is.

She's smiling at him, and her face still has some of that shocked-open look. She looks younger too, different. Her old self and new one at the same time. She chuckles, points to the withered plant on the desk.

"I bet someone gave her that!" she says and he'll never be able to explain why, or why then, but at that moment, hearing Marla laugh, Don starts to cry.

"Hey," she says, still smiling. But he can't smile back. Mouth, throat, lips—all of them seem to have a will of their own, and none of them want to coordinate.

"The thing is, it's just hit me." He sobs, wipes his face on his arms, tries again. "This is really dumb," he manages to say, taking her hands in his. "This is not the right thing to say. But I'll say it: I'll never know, Marla. I'll never know, now, how I would have been for you if—"

She hugs him until he pulls his head away.

Pigs

UNTIL THAT POINT, MIMI had approved of the hotel. It was a mixture of traditional and modern, with richly textured fabrics, above-average art, and well-chosen plants. Their room came with a traditional kiva fireplace and looked out onto a tree full of twittering birds. They were right downtown. Breakfast was in an ancient cellar, arches everywhere, lit with concealed fittings that brought out the colours of the exposed bricks. The buffet along the far side of the room ran the gamut from oatmeal and fruit to bacon, eggs, pastries and such, though of course Mimi was intending to stick to her plan, four hundred calories per meal. The room was full, but the server led them to a table for two in the middle, a round table covered with a red cloth and a piece of plate glass, perfectly clean. There were two upholstered *fauteuil*-style chairs with curved arms, modern but attractive. They seemed fairly generous.

The server took their order for coffee while they were still standing, and then they wove their way between the other diners to fetch glasses of juice from the buffet. This was quite stressful because the tables were so close together, but she only had to ask a couple of other guests to move in as she passed.

They returned to their table. Ken sat down. He did not seem to have any problem doing so, did not warn her, did not give her *any* kind of sign—and perhaps he even misled her. In any case, he sat down and smiled up at her, and, like a fool—or just hoping against hope, or just not thinking, forgetting who she was for whatever dumb reason—Mimi went to follow suit and the stupid chair arms dug into her buttocks in such a way that she knew that squeezing in was not a possibility. If she continued she'd be royally stuck, or break the damn thing, or both. As unobtrusively as possible she levered herself up, just as the server, a piece of string in a suit, reappeared and set their coffee press on the table.

"Is everything all right, madam?" he asked her, he and she the only two people standing in the room, complete opposites, what a lesson to the world. And at that moment, as she pointed out to him later, Ken seemed completely aware, because he looked the man in the face and said, with great authority, "That chair is too small. Please bring my wife a different one."

"Of course, sir," the server replied, and carried the chair away, holding it in front of himself like a walking frame. People were staring, naturally enough. The couple at the next table, for example, shot little glances her way between mouthfuls, then looked back at each other, making a fair number of assumptions, she was sure, and feeling some *schadenfreude*, a word they would not expect her to know—to them, "fat" meaning also greedy, lazy, and stupid—and feeling suddenly better about their own few extra pounds and sagging bits because there was now someone far worse to compare themselves with. Mimi would have walked back to the buffet for something to do while she waited, but her heart was racing and she didn't trust herself not to knock into someone or something, so she stayed put and watched Ken pour the coffee for both of them. He'd shaved well, had dressed in a navy tee that slimmed him down a bit and flattered his skin tone.

"Madam," said the server, setting down a padded dining chair with no sides, the best that could be expected, though of course her flesh, encased in stretchy black fabric, would be hanging over the edges of the seat.

"Thank you," she told him, and lowered herself carefully onto it. She kept her feet wide for balance.

"Is there anything else that you need?"

"No, thank you."

"Coffee's good," Ken said, pushing the cup towards her. She met his eyes and took a sip, feeling the steam on her face.

"Do you want me to get your breakfast?" he said. "What would you like?"

"Grapefruit," she told him. "An egg. Something delicious like that."

"Sure?" How could she eat anything else with a room full of people staring at her? She watched him use tongs to select a very white egg and slip it into the pottery egg cup, and add a piece of toast and then a half-grapefruit. He brought it over to her, then revisited the buffet for his own food, returning with bacon, sausages, beans and scrambled eggs, two toasts, and a pastry.

The half-grapefruit had been prepared well and was of the pink kind, so not too sour or hard to get at. She was soon done with that and the egg, and she left half of the toast: total consumption about two hundred calories. Ken, on the other hand, had over a thousand to absorb. She watched him eat quite slowly, dabbing his lips with the napkin from time to time. Was it good? she asked. Yes, he told her, very. She wasn't envious; she preferred subtler tastes and sweeter things and, anyway, her appetite had—temporarily—vanished. At the end, he took one bite out of his miniature Danish and then offered it to her. She declined and he placed it abstemiously on his napkin.

It was as they left the breakfast room that she thought she heard someone say, quietly, not intending them to hear, *pigs*. She made it up the brick stairs to the lobby, then burst into tears. Ken held her hand in the elevator.

In their room, she lay face down on the bed, sobbing. Her new lilac tee-shirt was damp, her face sticky with tears. So unfair! she told Ken, pushing herself up into a sitting position. How dare they? What made them think they could say such a thing? What did they know? She hardly ate! And who knew what awful things they did that just didn't show! And why the hell didn't he warn her about that chair?

"Mimi, I can't always be thinking for you," Ken said, and disappeared into the bathroom.

"Did you do it on purpose?" she shouted at the closed door. He didn't reply. She could hear him peeing. Then a silence.

"I think you did!" she continued. "Just because you're stabilized, you think you're better than me! You're not, do you hear me? You're not! Remember, you're the one who made me like this, you bastard!"

In the silence that followed this, she heard the flush of the toilet, the rush of the faucet, then the buzzing of his toothbrush. He was ignoring her. She had to forgive him when he did this, and other cruel things, because he was as ashamed as she was. Hurting her made him feel better.

"I want to make absolutely clear that I am not going to tell you what to do," Dr. Carmel had told Mimi, and it seemed like an excellent start, seeing as everyone else she had consulted had done so very much of that: admit this, list that, set such-and-such a supposedly realistic goal, count this, avoid this, weigh that, exercise with *x* much intensity for so many hours at *y* heart rate, record everything that passes your lips in an eating diary, weigh and measure and photograph yourself, calculate, draw a graph, remember that you are an addict and must act accordingly, and do all this while faint with hunger and more miserable every passing day.

Dr. Carmel's office contained no hectoring posters, no scales and no mirrors. Instead, there was a choice of comfortable seating, along with cool, filtered water, tissues, soft lights and some contemporary prints on the walls. Carmel herself, although a size four at most, didn't flaunt it. She had rosy cheeks, corkscrew curls and bird-bright brown eyes. "I have no stake in you changing your behaviour," she explained, her voice lively without being obtrusive. "Our aim is simple: for you to be fully aware of the choices you have made and continue to make. Do you want to fill me in on the background?"

Mimi explained that she had always been chubby due to her sweet tooth and preference for Western foods. "But I was only 180 and five-four when I met Ken," she said. Now she was three hundred. "My mother is tiny and still eats the traditional Japanese way. She was always on at me and it only made things worse. 'You'll never get married,' et cetera. Ken and I met at a conference. He was about 280, five-seven. Substantial. He's still in that zone, yo-yos around if the doctor scares him. And he's diabetic, but I'm not. Ken liked me how I was, and we enjoyed cooking and eating out together, so I just gave up on all that dieting and anxiety. He was successful in his business. We started to travel. We got married after a year or so. It was all pretty liberating, and he kept on liking me however I was. And sex was pretty good for a few years, too."

"And now?" Carmel had asked. Ten years and a hundred pounds on, they still sometimes managed the full works. Last night, even. Lots of pillows to get the angle. A big woman, no longer young, looks her best lying down but even so, she was fat everywhere and it got in the way. They'd lost some depth. He couldn't actually see himself going into her, which was part of the turn-on for him, and of late he'd taken to wanting some dirty talk while they did it. *Say it: "I'm a fat, dirty bitch, please fuck me now."* You weren't supposed to mind that sort of thing, but, in all honesty, she did. And a belly gets in the way of your head. So, fingers, mostly. Nice enough, if hard work (though what isn't?). And now, the morning after, here she was on this hotel bed in Santa Fe—faint with hunger, having been called a pig—while he brushed his teeth and ignored her. Yet he had happily agreed to come here just because she wanted to see Georgia O'Keeffe's house, and he *still* said he liked her exactly how she was. He had *never* suggested she try to slim down. "You have an appetite," he'd once told her, "and that's a good thing. You can't resist, or don't want to. You're going to say yes, not no. I like that." Even so, he wasn't always kind. Sometimes she hated him.

They had no children, and no doctor prepared to help. Ken said he didn't mind. She'd had to abandon her interior design consultancy. Once she could no longer dress well, it was over, no matter how good her work. No new clients, old ones melting away. She had tried, very hard, to get back to her old size, and she had failed. *Don't worry,* Ken told her. He was fine: a fat realtor doesn't seem such an issue, not if he's a guy. Look at it as an opportunity, he'd said. You don't have to work.

She took up painting in acrylics and helped Ken with staging. They had several investment properties, as well as their own place in Burlington. They'd lost a bit, of course, but things would bounce back eventually. They brought in help for the house and the yardwork. It was a good life, though Mimi's mother, who visited once or twice a year, still hadn't given up: *You were a beautiful baby. Why have you denied me grandchildren? What did I do wrong?*

Don't listen, Ken always said. Let it wash over you. Same as he did to her.

She opened the drawer and took out a bright silk scarf from the Uffizi Gallery in Florence and a black tee-shirt from Making It Big.

"Hurry up, now," she called to Ken. Her heart was racing. "I want to change, and then we need to get moving. It's fifty miles away and we have to be on time."

He emerged from the bathroom in time to help her tug the lilac tee off, and then he ran his hand slowly over the folds of skin on her back. Touch: how could she ever be without that? The more skin you have, the more you can feel. That's what it seemed like to her. She wept a bit into his shoulder, then put on the fresh shirt and squeezed into the bathroom.

"I've been checking out where we can go for dinner," Ken said as she emerged.

"Are you fully aware of the health risks involved in being morbidly obese?" Dr. Carmel had asked in the same warm, spirited tone she used for pleasantries at the beginning of a session. Mimi felt she was fairly aware, yes. She knew what refined sugar did to her metabolism, had heard of the Glycaemic Index, of the effects of good fats and bad fats. She understood how the fat cells in her body both grew and multiplied, had been told that they could burst under pressure and create lipotoxicity in her system. She was aware of the stress her liver was under (Ken's too), of the likely effects on her mental clarity and mood. She was aware of all this, but since it was so very hard to change she preferred not to dwell on it, and in any case, now, as they drove through a landscape of ochres, pinks and greens against a clear blue sky her mood was very positive.

As instructed, they parked at the visitor centre in Abiquiu, checked in, and transferred to the minivan. The steps were awkward, but she took the roomier seat right at the front and Ken squeezed into the one behind her. There were only six others on the tour: two Germans, a Canadian, a middle-aged woman wearing a lot of jewellery, and a moody-looking younger couple in faded, flowing clothes. She and Ken were the only people not sporting serious walking shoes. Before they set off, the guide, Rosa, explained that that cameras, cellphones, and sketching were all banned at the house; they were to experience the place through their own senses, with no distractions. *And buy their expensive postcards after*, Ken muttered into Mimi's ear as the bus coughed into life.

At the other end of the ride, Mimi waited until everyone else had left and climbed carefully out of the van. It was hot now and very bright, a faint herbal tang to the air. The vast landscape spread out beyond them, utterly unlike home.

The group approached the house through a garden that was just beginning to show signs of growth: onions, spinach, lettuce and carrots. They paused there while Rosa gave them a few details: the traditional construction of the house, the irrigation of the garden, O'Keeffe's first trip to the area in 1929, her lengthy campaign to buy this particular property, her eventual purchase of the place, as a ruin, in 1949, a few years after the death of her husband, Stieglitz, and the careful restoration she carried out. She had lived there until she was in her nineties. The guide used to be one of her housekeepers.

They moved inside to the kitchen: white enamelled units, stove and sink against white walls, a pale wooden table, a bare bulb, and, of course, the view.

O'Keeffe, arguably the best and best-known woman artist ever, was tiny. A bony face. Strong hands. Self-sufficient and focused, but not, Mimi thought, a self-starver. She was very active, walked many miles a day. According to Rosa, she had enjoyed her food and been a great cook, or supervisor of cooks—one who favoured healthy organic food, locally grown. But she did enjoy desserts, too. She liked to say that something was *scandalously good*. They were shown her neatly arranged pots and pans, were allowed to peer into her pantry and examine a shelf of well-used recipe books.

From there, they progressed to the studio, its light and views, the huge homemade table. In her later years, as she lost her sight, O'Keeffe had turned to sculpture.

Many of the rooms were out of bounds, but they could examine them through doorways or windows. They could see the small single bed the artist slept in decade after decade, the land formations and desert colours that greeted her when she woke up, the rocks and bones she had collected, so simple and beautiful that they made Mimi want to weep.

As for the chairs, not one of which Mimi could have sat in, even if it had been allowed, there was a black bucket affair with a footstool, very elegant, and something else upholstered in a dark orange that looked like

Eames. A squarish, nondescript thing in the bedroom. She was studying that through the window when the Canadian woman came up to her and said, "Isn't it wonderful! Such a life! Stieglitz was a mixed blessing, though, don't you think?"

"Excuse me?"

"He made her what she was, of course, but he stopped her from being what she might have been. Suppose she had been a mother, for example. Who knows what that would have done to her work. Why did he assume it would be bad?"

"I don't know," Mimi said, looking for Ken, who had slipped back into the kitchen.

The group met in the indoor patio for questions.

"Suppose Georgia had never met Stieglitz," the Canadian asked. "Would we know about her now?"

"I think so, yes," the guide replied, "though she would probably not have achieved commercial success so early on. She would have struggled more, and produced less."

"In all those years after her husband died," asked a leathery looking woman wearing white linen and an elaborate silver and turquoise necklace, "did Georgia have any other romantic relationships?"

"I can't comment on that," Rosa said, "except to say that she was a person who did only what she wanted to do. She was very content with the interpersonal connections in her life, and she was, of course, totally focused on her work."

"What about her assistant, Juan? Wasn't there something going on there?" asked the female half of the bohemian-looking couple. With great aplomb, Rosa ignored her and looked around in case someone else was going to speak. Mimi longed to ask a question: How come Georgia O'Keeffe was so strong and focused, and I am so weak and edgeless? What is missing in me? How come she made what she wanted of her life, and I have just become something half by accident? What would I be like if I had not met Ken? Suppose I did lose weight, would I paint any better? She was well aware that these questions were not appropriate and didn't ask them, but Ken had no such inhibitions.

"Rosa," he said, "suppose you could take O'Keeffe right out of this place and look at it as just a restored courtyard house with an older kitchen. Can you give me a ballpark figure as to what the value of the property would be today?"

"You can't take Georgia O'Keeffe out of this house," Rosa said, frowning, "or even out of the state. This area is desirable because of her. I advise you to consult a realtor. Thank you, everyone, for coming on this tour."

"I could find out on my phone right now, if I was allowed to look," Ken said as they made their way out. "About five hundred thousand is my guess. I'm sorry," he told her as they approached the van. "I know you love her paintings, and, sure, they're original. But the saintly vibe gets me all riled up."

In the third session, Dr. Carmel had suggested they look at the costs of taking action versus the costs of not doing so. The loss of her job and the deterioration in her sex life had already been noted. On top of that, staying big computed to losing five years of life expectancy, and there were plenty of impacts on her quality of life: chronic problems such as deteriorating joints, things like hiking and cycling that she could no longer do, the way she felt about herself, the way she was seen and judged by others—social detriment, Dr. Carmel called the latter. As for choosing to lose, Mimi had surprised herself by saying, "If I want to lose, I might have to also lose Ken, because he might not like me if I wasn't this way. He always says people our size who diet look worse than they did before." They suffered for it, too: the swathes of stretched skin, the surgeries—another cost. Suppose she made that choice and he didn't like it, could she exist on her own? Would anyone but Ken ever love her? These, Carmel said, were fears and risks, not costs.

She felt faint as they got into the bus. The Canadian woman and the hippie couple were going on to do the Ghost Ranch tour and hike, and it seemed that almost everyone else in the party had already done so. There was talk of visits to Plaza Blanca, and the archaeological sites at Tsankawi, both of which sounded worth seeing, but not in the midday heat. Ken wanted lunch and bought a sandwich at the visitor centre. Mimi didn't want one. Just some water, she said. Her knees hurt because of all the standing.

What's the matter? he asked as they climbed into the car. She did not answer, but put her hand on his leg. He drove with one hand on the wheel while he ate.

We are killing each other, Mimi thought. Or killing ourselves, together.

They took a different, much longer way home, beginning on the 96 before turning onto the 550 and passing through many hypnotic and empty miles of sagebrush and juniper, with purplish hills to the left and the occasional patch of forest—O'Keeffe country, as it was called, the sky above dotted with small, puffy clouds. Mimi let her hand rest on Ken's leg and listened to song after song until she fell asleep.

That night, they walked to one of the trendier of the restaurants in town for tapas. Mimi was, by then, very hungry—she had hardly eaten all day—and the tiny plates, each bearing a different salty, interesting morsel, were both strange and delicious. They tasted ingenious combinations of meat, fish and leaves, and risotto flavoured with unknown herbs and garnished with pomegranate, flower petals, and curls of orange peel, or studded with locally gathered pine nuts.

Yet before long, she was full and sleepy again from the wine.

"Do you want to go on to another place?" Ken asked. "I could certainly fit in something a little more substantial."

On the way out, they passed the couple who had been sitting next to them at breakfast, the pair who had discreetly watched Mimi struggle with her chair and afterwards eat her horrible egg, who had made her their morning entertainment. She did not think it was one of them who had said *pigs*, though she could not be sure. Now they were coming into the restaurant just as she and Ken left it. Mimi and the woman made eye contact. The woman smiled—falsely, Mimi assumed—and they each nodded at the other.

I would not want to be like you, dull and disciplined and closed-minded, Mimi thought, even if it meant living five more years.

Ken stopped and bought a takeout pizza on the way back. After Ken had spent some time emailing and eating it, they turned in early, both exhausted: the effect of the thin air, they decided, as much as the events of the day. Yet she woke a few hours later, her heart pounding, Ken snoring heavily beside her. The room seemed stuffy and too small, and it was impossible to fall asleep again. Ken's wet-sounding snores built up to a periodic crisis, at which point he made a startled choking sound and almost woke. Before they'd left for the holiday, he had ordered some kind of machine that was supposed to help.

We are killing each other, she thought again. By inches. Or mouthfuls. Sometimes deliciously, but not always so. They were killing each other routinely, sometimes grudgingly or argumentatively, and mostly they were unaware of what they were doing. But now, she could see it, the strangeness of the pact they were joined in without ever having discussed it or consented to its goals or terms. Gravity pulled down on every pound of her flesh. She was her own worst enemy, and his. Time and time again his breath rattled through his constricted airways. Suppose, she thought. Suppose. A pillow on his face. He was stronger than her, but she had more bulk, the advantage of surprise.

Bees

We were waiting for the 159 bus. I wore my blue tee-shirt and my smart buff trousers with the crease: clean, but they didn't go together. Belinda had put on my white tee-shirt and a flowery tie-round skirt. She was trying to grow her hair but it just got thicker. She looked about fifteen. I looked about forty. We had the shopping cart with us.

If there had been an office worker or a stay-at-home wife at the bus stop they'd have looked away, steered clear of us, and that's the sort of thing which back then used to piss me right off, but now I just think: okay. Because the fact is, a person's qualities aren't visible from outside. To give an example: I know, because I did some tests once at the university (they pay you for it), that I've a very good memory for details—total recall, more or less. No one on earth could spot that just from looking at me, and that's an obvious thing, not a complicated one, such as: I think sometimes that I see things the same way an artist does. I can imagine myself leading a revolution, or stealing a famous painting just to keep it in my living room, or jumping out of an airplane with only the silk of a parachute to keep me safe. From the outside, no one would guess any of this, not in a thousand years. And maybe I wouldn't want them to.

For weeks I had been looking out for a fridge, and I had a feeling that I would find it that morning. It was more of a seeing than a feeling. I could picture the kind of street: smart, but not so smart that the neighbours complained if you left something outside. Fresh white paint. Plane trees. The houses would have small patches of garden in the front, where people kept their bins behind a hedge. The fences and walls would be low. Some of the houses would be split into flats, some would have converted attics. Wrought iron gates, window boxes, new roofs, entry phones, burglar alarms, *Residents Only Parking*. You get a nose for the right kind of place eventually, just as you can roughly tell by looking at it whether a cast-off electrical appliance will work or not.

Daley is a practical person, useful, optimistic and a good contributor to any team: Mrs. de Soto wrote that for my reference. People often patronize someone in my situation, but you learn to sift the wheat from the chaff, and that one is definitely true.

A bus came, but it was a 3. Never mind.

"I hope something good happens today," Belinda said. She was fidgeting and her face was ghost-white from lack of sleep.

"It will," I said, thinking of the fridge. "Cheer up."

We'd met a month before. I was passing and I helped her to break down the door of an empty seventh-floor flat on the Beveridge estate. I don't think squatting is wrong. I came inside to see if there was anything else needed. Right from the start she didn't really like the place, but I said: later on you can find something better, but what you need right now is a roof over your head and a door you can bolt behind you. It was clean, the plumbing still in.

I went to buy a new lock, and on the way back I saw a cooker in a skip. The next day I met a bloke who could wire the electricity from the corridor for a tenner. I found a rug, a kettle and a not-bad mattress, so I took them over too.

She said she's not told anyone before, but her uncle interfered with her. I told her I can sympathize because I've not had much what you'd call positive sexual experience myself: just once with an older girl at the home, when I was twelve. A member of staff found us and I got shut up on my own for a week.

Belinda said I was a good listener. It was late when we finished talking, so I stayed. We wore our clothes in bed. I made sure not to touch her at all because it had to be that way. Come morning, I made tea.

"Don't go," she said. So I went to check out at Dempsey House. Mrs. de Soto told me that they wouldn't automatically take me back again if it didn't work out with Belinda. I didn't care. I hadn't had the chance to live with someone out of choice before and I thought it would be paradise.

But Belinda couldn't stop her mind from going round in circles and felt shut in. I said, let's scout around and see if there is anywhere else, and at the same time, I thought, I'll keep my eye out for a fridge—and that's how come we were there waiting for the 159, which, the fact is, you wait for a lot.

"Daley," Belinda said, "I want a garden. I need space." She has no idea what's possible and what's not. But I wanted to keep things sweet so I said I didn't see why we shouldn't have a garden, and then she put her arm around me, which by then meant I could do the same to her.

I knew how to treat Belinda from being in the Group. They encouraged you to get feelings out of your system, even if you didn't know they were there: bashing cushions, running around on all fours yelling and screaming. I thought *Christ!* when I started, but it was more embarrassing not to, and after a couple of weeks I was in there with the best. Sometimes my throat ached for days afterwards, and I'd have this strange, empty feeling as if I'd just arrived from Mars. Once the bloke who ran the group, Ian, took me into his arms and hugged me and it really stirred me up. But the fact is, that kind of professional person may do an excellent job but they only care about you so much. It is not the same as an actual relationship.

"Something backing onto a park, maybe. I'd be okay then," Belinda said.

"Sounds good." I said, although I knew there was sod all chance of us squatting a place like that unless it had rotten floors, no windows, a rodent problem. Even then it would be someone's investment, biding its time: they would get us out, just like that.

Belinda flung her hand out to stop the bus. We went top front. I put my feet on the ledge and thought more about our fridge. How it would be standing at the edge of the road ready to be taken away—a big fridge with a separate freezer at the top. It would fit just so on the cart. If the conductor kicked up I would walk it back, and Belinda would meet me at the other end. Once we had a fridge, we could do a bulk shop when our cheques came through. I saw Belinda and me pushing a cart round a huge supermarket, stopping to decide how many tins of tomatoes to buy. The aisles stretched out in front of us: Tea and Coffee, Dairy, Tinned Goods, Butter, Delicatessen, Hot Bread Shop, Fruit and Vegetables, Pasta, Juices, Condiments, et cetera. Steam wafting above the freezer cabinets. I would have a list, the meals all planned out, but occasionally we'd buy off-the-cuff: some strange kind of sausage or milky-fruity pudding thing or a spiny-looking fruit that made your mouth wrinkle, but it was worth finding out or you'd always hanker after knowing.

I'm not greedy but I do have an appetite for making decisions. This above that, have this and wait for that. Two of these, three of those and none of that, thanks. Which size? Which colour? Good value? *Daley is happy to take on responsibilities*, the woman from Social Services once wrote. Well, true—but, with respect, there's more to me than people like her ever saw.

The picture of us among all that food gave me a lump in my throat. I imagined that we were smarter dressed and I was younger and she was wearing lipstick, though for the life of me I don't think she ever will.

The fridge would just fit into the niche on the left of the kitchen. When we got in, I would load it up, fitting everything on the shelves just so. I have a certificate in food hygiene, with distinction (not that it's proved as useful as they said), and I would keep it properly clean. *Everything he does, he does thoroughly and with care*, the teacher wrote on my leaving report, and again, it's true.

Belinda dug me in the ribs and said how if we got a house with a garden we could grow vegetables and live off the land like the people we'd seen in a programme on TV.

"All the waste could be returned to the soil," she said. "I wonder how much land you need to be self-sufficient?" She looked at me as if I would be bound to know.

"A lot," I said. The bus turned onto the main road and picked up speed. Shops and offices flashed by.

"We could grow vegetables and have a goat. We could make the milk into cheese." People don't have goats in cities. I heard of a woman once who kept a rabbit in a flat and it died of eating carpet. Also goats stink and so does the milk and it would probably eat the garden. How would you get hold of one anyway? I couldn't see it. But I kept quiet.

"We could have open fires," she said, "for heating and cooking. We could collect wood from skips."

"The chimneys would need seeing to, then," I said, "and cooking on an open fire is not easy, unless you want to get food poisoning." I could see I was being a wet blanket, so for balance I added that some kind of solid fuel range might be better.

"Candlelight," she said. "I don't want electricity."

"What about the TV?'" I asked. We had one in the flat—another thing I'd found. A big Sony in a mahogany cabinet, nothing wrong with it at all. "The TV would need electricity, and the fridge-freezer."

"I don't want a fridge," she said, then added, "I'd rather have things fresh out of the garden."

"You can't live on greens," I told her. "What about meat? What about winter?" I started to get tense, which I hadn't in a long time. A pulse beat in the back of my eyes. When I shut them, all I could see was the fridge, almost new. I could hear it hum.

"We'll be vegetarians," I heard her say, "though we could have chickens for the eggs."

"You don't know what you're talking about!" I said. And now the bus was stuck in a jam. Everything smelled of diesel. I kept my eyes tight shut. "A vegetarian diet is complicated. Believe me, I know. You need to get the balance right, the proteins, minerals, vitamins. And what are we supposed to do in winter, living off this garden, if we can't freeze things?"

"They managed before there were freezers," she said. "They bottled things." At that, I opened my eyes.

"Who the fuck is going to bottle things?" I said. I never swear.

"Me," she said. It struck me for the first time that since we'd been sharing, Belinda had barely lifted a finger. She didn't do much at all.

"Oh yes?" I said. "I'd rather not die of botulism."

"What? Anyway, we haven't got a fridge—or a garden," she said. "This is stupid."

"I want a fridge," I said, turning to her, jabbing my finger at my chest to underline the words. My face burned.

"You want such ordinary things," she said in a bored voice. The bus was still stuck. Something was going on in the street ahead and she stared at it, ignoring me.

"No!" I said. "Nothing feels ordinary to me. And anyway, what's wrong with ordinary? You're pretty ordinary, and I want you."

"Oh, just fuck off, Dale," she said, pushing past me. She strode back and took the stairs down, then got right off the bus.

I watched her cross to the opposite pavement. She didn't look back. I sat there, stunned, running the conversation through to see where it went wrong. I had gone as far as I could with her garden idea, but it just wasn't practical. At the same time I had to admit that the feeling I had about the fridge had swayed me. The fridge was almost human, the way I felt about it. It was stupid to care so much about something that didn't exist; then again, we both did that. We both kept pictures in our heads, kept adding to them. I could see that now. It was something that joined us.

And then I was off the bus and running after her, my heart banging in my chest. I could just see her, bobbing down the street. I had forgotten the shopping cart! Too late. I'm not used to running.

"Belinda!" I yelled.

It might half-work, I thought. Even suppose we stayed in the flat but got hold of an allotment—people do. A waiting list, no doubt. But still: she'd do the gardening, grow what she could, and I'd do what I'm good at, find things, to make up the difference. When we had what we needed I'd start selling. Appliances are one thing; the real money these days is in antiques. Glass lampshades, doorknobs, patterned finger plates, letterboxes, bell pushes, bits of wrought iron. There's plenty of empty private houses. You can't squat them but they're stuffed with things like that. All you need is a screwdriver. A market stall. A van. Then I could go for the bigger things—fireplaces, cast iron baths, panelled doors. Architectural salvage, it's called. It might half-work, if she could accept the compromise. I might even end up with a shop.

"Belinda, please, stop!" I called as I saw her hesitate then disappear into a crowd that had gathered by the railway bridge. Maybe she really meant it when she said she'd do the bottling and so on. Why not? Maybe she wanted to pull her weight, and what had I done? Squabble over a fridge! It wasn't true about her being ordinary. I thought how she might just wander off and then I'd be back to square one or worse, just as they'd warned me at Dempsey House.

I knew that's how she'd go. She wouldn't warn you. No discussions. She'd wander off and all I'd be left with would be an ache. She must have wandered off from somewhere when I first met her, and even now I didn't know exactly where from.

"Belinda!" I shouted. "Wait!" I pushed into the crowd. People were turned in a kind of circle. I squeezed my way through. I couldn't see what was going on: some kind of fight. I don't like violence. Christ, I thought, I'll never get out of here. But there she was on the other side, striding down the street. The traffic coming towards us was stuck, too. A police car zoomed up the middle of the road. And finally, I caught up.

"Belinda!" I said. She kept walking but she slowed down.

"What pisses me off is that the things you want are easier to get than the things I want," she said after we had gone a little way. She still wouldn't look at me. She was chewing her lip. "Most of the things I want are impossible. It isn't fair."

By then we'd got to another bus stop. We sat down on the bench there and I told her how I had thought everything through. I'd added bits by then. For instance, I told her, I thought we might well be able to keep bees, even here in the city. I'd read somewhere that there are more flowers in city gardens than in the whole of the countryside put together.

It was a day for seeing things and I saw a white wooden hive. I saw fat, stripey bees buzzing and crawling on a sticky comb, and I saw the honey dripping into a big glass jar. It was the colour of strong tea before the milk goes in, a dark, reddish brown, clear and glowing. I told Belinda everything, until I ran out of words, and when she kissed me on the mouth, it was as if she was turning me gently inside out to look for something she had lost.

It is July Now

I RODE THE BUS TO THE AIRPORT so as to keep the expenses for myself. It took an hour and a half, and then the plane was forty-five minutes late. Naturally, I do not take kindly to extra work at weekends, and for two weeks the Director has been plaguing me to inspect the flat—and before that, he rejected one I had found myself: one room only and landlady in situ would not, he said, be suitable for a visitor. They are used to having personal space, he said. A flat is a flat, I thought. Four walls. I did not make the inspection, but I told the Director that I had.

"Some of the people in our academy," I told the Director when he first suggested I have a visitor in my department, "are the foremost experts in their fields and it is a joy to hear them speak. But many of the foreigners who come do not even use their own languages correctly, let alone have a proper pedagogical method! They say that they are very interested in us and would rather be here than at home, but it is my view that some of them come because there is unemployment in their own countries and they are inadequate to secure proper positions. So I am against it."

"Even so," he said, clicking his pen in and out, as he does, "there is nothing to be lost." So it was decided.

Just as I was convinced that she had missed the plane, I turned around, and the person sitting on the bench behind me, wearing a dark red coat with gold buttons and no hat, could only be her. I could see at once that the coat was far too long. It will trail in the mud, I thought. The shoes will be soaked through. And her hair was cut short about her face so that she looked like a child, but with very shiny lipstick on: the fashion, perhaps, where she comes from, but to my mind not a good one. Fashion is an odd business. There, where they have freedom, they follow it. Here, where there has been none, we are all individuals.

"Good afternoon," I said.

"Hello." She stood up, her gloves fell to the ground and she bent straight down to pick them up, forgetting to offer her hand.

The Director had said that I should invite her to my home. A glass of wine with cheese was the done thing, he told me. I have a whole house, only a minute from the city centre but built in the country style. Three floors, four rooms, a garden, gables. I had it painted ice-cream pink last summer. It is large enough for my daughter, Katrin, and I not to get in each other's skirts. She has a job at the city hall but still they won't allocate her a flat because there is enough space here. Still, I have my own study in the attic, with waxed floors, fresh curtains, a good rug, a proper office chair and a telephone extension. The house is mine—nationalized, of course, but I have the proofs and it is just a matter of time—and *even you*, I thought at the Director, cannot compel me to have someone in it if I do not want. He is young, very clever. Before, he was a scholar in a garret. Now he has been given a laptop computer, whereas I am paid nothing extra for being Head of Department, though it looks good on my curriculum vitae, which we all have to have now—and eventually, when this country is sorted out it may lead to something.

The flat is in an anonymous district on the outskirts of town, big blocks with numbers and no names, and because I haven't been there before I'm unable to give good directions. The taxi driver is Russian and loses patience so I decide it is better to walk. She has some boots, she says, but they are right at the bottom of her bag. Should she get them out? I tell her no.

"This isn't what I imagined," she says. "What sort of place is it?"

"It is typical of where people live," I tell her. Finally we arrive. The stairs smell terrible. Still, I think, it will probably be all right inside.

"I have never seen so many cats!" she exclaims.

"Actually, I have a cat myself," I say, as I try to let us in—the lock is stiff. "It is on penicillin at the moment," I tell her. "Extremely expensive, an import. People can look after themselves, and wild animals, but pets are helpless. We must take care of them."

Finally the door opens on a narrow corridor with a room either side and the bathroom at the end. The place is extremely hot and dusty. I go straight to open a window, also stuck, and when I get it opened I see that there are an old cupboard and some rotting rugs on the balcony, and the remains of a seagull in the middle of it all. I remember also that I had told the visiting lecturer that I had inspected the accommodation and that it was acceptable.

She walks around, trying everything in a curious kind of way, even pulling open the kitchen drawers and flushing the toilet. The television does not work.

"In any case, it would be incomprehensible," I tell her.

"Well, not the pictures," she points out.

"The programmes are of poor quality. It wouldn't interest you. Here are your fees for the three weeks." She looks at the money, puts it back in the envelope without counting it, undoes her coat. She has on a pair of close-fitting black trousers and soft brown sweater. She stretches her arms and rolls her head around.

"What next?" she says. It is dark by now. I take her straight out to look at the shop and the bus stop and tell her that I will meet her at Kaarmanni Õlletuba at eight for supper; the Academy will pay. Just then my bus comes. Anyone will know where it is, I tell her as I get on.

She wants me to write some phrases down for her.

"Really, there is no point in language lessons," I say. I have put on my suit and a brooch. She too has changed, and it is a cream knitted dress now, with flecks of grey and red in it and a roll neck. "You will learn nothing in such a short time; it is extremely complex, grammatically."

"I'm not talking grammar," she says. "I just want to be able to point at a sandwich and say please. Or, for instance, to say, 'Can you give me directions to' rather than just barking the name of a café at some poor woman in a bus. Do you see what I mean, Piret?" She has a habit of using one's name all the time.

"You are here for just three weeks," I say. "Everyone can see that you are a stranger. They won't expect it of you."

"That's not the point," she insists. I am not used to being argued with.

"We have a great deal to do," I say. We push on and cover the necessary arrangements for the coming weeks. I am quite ready to go then, but she is still drinking her soup like a snail.

"Well, Piret," she says, very informally, "tell me about yourself."

"Here," I tell her, "—we do not have small talk here. We get to know each other slowly."

"I see," she says. She plays with her bread and looks around her as if trying to commit the place to memory. "Could we have more wine?" she asks—and that uses up the money I have saved by coming on the bus.

"Life is hard," I tell her while we drink it. "It cannot be legislated against as you are always trying to in the West. You have a deal—good parents, bad parents, dead parents, a good country, a bad country or in-between. However it is, you use your talents to carve a way for yourself. You just make the best of it. Some people go under. Some people complain too much. Others are too kind..." Drink makes me talk. When at last we emerge, there is a strong wind blowing from the sea; the thermometer in the square shows minus fifteen. "What is your word for snow?" she asks.

At home, Katrin is still up, eating milk pudding and watching the Finnish television channel, very loud, and reading magazines at the same time. The magazines are dreadful. What is your wildest dream? they ask. Do you get enough? How do you rate on the passion scale? She is not an intellectual, though she could have been. Perhaps it is to spite me. She is particularly difficult these days. You resent me! she accuses.

It's not my fault there's an accommodation shortage. At least, I tell her when she complains, you have a mother, which I did not for very long—all I remember is her brushing my hair, and coming to me in the night. I dream of that still, once in a while; it's only natural. My father, of course, was away in the war, then died in it.

Mainly I grew up in the orphanage—it was harsh, but invaluable in teaching self-reliance.

I didn't ask to be born, Katrin is always saying. You think you've done such a lot for me but you haven't. I want nothing from you. You've never really loved me, it's only duty.

She becomes impassioned. You think he would have stayed with you, happy ever after, if not for me, she says. Don't you?

We make our meals separately now. After all, she is twenty-five. Some of what she says is true, but not all.

The visiting lecturer came ten minutes late to the department in the morning. Apparently, the night before, she had left the bus at the wrong stop and had to walk several kilometres through the snow, and then there was some problem with the toilet in her flat, which flooded; also she said drunken men had banged on the door in the small hours. "But this is normal," I told her, "in the district where you are." She was wearing jeans and a silk blouse, like a student, very odd. She spent the morning photocopying and used most of the paper for the term.

I do not normally go out with subordinates, but a visitor has ambiguous status so I accepted her invitation to attend a concert.

"Let me treat you," she said.

"Here, each of us must keep to her own economy," I pointed out. "It is simply too stressful otherwise. It is almost rude to suggest such a thing. You will embarrass people. They will feel that they have to return a favour when they simply cannot afford it."

"I'm sorry," she said, and blushed.

As we left the concert, which thankfully put no one to shame, she asked if she could have a favour.

"I need to call home," she told me, "and none of the boxes do international calls, or am I missing something? But the phones at the Academy would do it, I think. Do you possibly have a key? If that's not possible, maybe you have the right kind of telephone yourself, at home?"

It was urgent, she said, and I did not feel I could reasonably refuse, so we went to the Academy, which seemed eerie without students and colleagues there. Our footsteps echoed in the corridors. It was hard to find the light switches. I gave up and waited in the dark on a bench in the corridor while she used the departmental phone. I could hear her voice but not the words. It rose and fell and there were long silences, exclamations, laughter. This was not business, and it was not urgent. Twenty-five minutes passed before she emerged, a half-smile on her lips, her eyes shining. When Katrin wears that kind of face, she always avoids questions and goes straight to her room.

"You have dealt with the matter?"

"Oh yes, thanks Piret," she said, smiling.

And I could not sleep all night. I kept thinking of Karel, Katrin's father. We were both students. It was the last year when we grew close. In summer we were both sent to do compulsory training in medical studies so that we could fulfil our obligations if war broke out. It was in the forest, lectures all day, anatomy and so forth, but the nights were mainly our own and they were long, warm nights. We swam in the lake together, while others drank and sang patriotic songs; we despised them. Out there, beyond the reach of their voices, the water was smooth and cool as glass, and afterwards our bodies were like silk. At this point I remember thinking that so long as you knew someone else who thought like you, anything was tolerable. Across whatever horrors, you could hold to that connection. When we got back, he came every night to my flat. It was not deliberately that I became pregnant, but I do not believe in interfering with what is meant to be. And I do not believe in being trapped if there is something that can be done to prevent it, Karel said. He took up a post in the North before she was born and I never heard from him again. I don't think of him often now.

The cat climbed onto my bed. It wheezed when it purred but otherwise seemed all right. I smoothed down its fur and it stretched out flat with its ears back, so very comforting. I could hear Katrin snoring at the other side of the house. She has done so since a child, and to start with, I tried to cure her of it by waking her, but finally I gave up.

Next it is the post office. I have given directions, but she insists on being taken there. She insists also on having her letters weighed so that they cost four times what they would have. "Just put the stamp on," I told her. "Are they going to sit at the airport checking each one?"

"Maybe that's why your last to me never arrived," she says, but the fact is I had not got around to writing it. I excuse myself from lunch. There are some cheese pies at home and I want to check the cat. The vet said that with this virus, the medicine might strengthen him but the cure will depend on his natural resistance. Katrin thinks I care more about that cat than I do about her. She says I never made a fuss over her, though of course that is not true, it is just that she does not remember. It is an instinct to be tender with children, something that happens whether you will it or not. Children who have their parents take things for granted. She says that I love the cat in a way I never loved her. She says that the money I spend on it, added up, would get her a plane ticket anywhere in Europe. She means Paris: a Frenchman came with a trade delegation. She has many boyfriends. However, I do not allow them to stay in the house.

"This country is supposed to be liberated!" she tells me. "There is nowhere for us to go. You are a greedy, jealous old woman!" Sometimes, when I get in, I have a sense that someone else has been in the house, though there is never any proof. I feel the cat knows too.

Towards the end of her last week, the visiting lecturer waits outside in the corridor for me to finish my Level Three lesson and asks, for the fourth time, to go to lunch together.

"Somewhere cheap," she says. "We'll go Dutch of course."

"But actually, I am going home for lunch today," I say. "Dutch?"

"Well I can't go home," she says. "It takes an hour each way on the bus. You could stretch a point."

"Is there a reason?" I say. "Is there some particular academic matter you wish to discuss?"

"No," she says, "there isn't. Just some food and a chat. For the sake of itself." None of my regular lecturers would suggest such a thing.

"Perhaps," I tell her, "I can organize it so that we go out for a drink on your last night, along with the Director, who would be interested to hear what you think about our students and their progress. I can call him this afternoon and make arrangements."

"No." She stares at me. "I was asking you, Piret, whether you wanted lunch, with me, now."

"I have told you."

"You," she said, "take the biscuit."

"The biscuit?"

"This is a one-way street," she says. Again, I query the idiom. "There is no point in language lessons," she says. Her voice turns hard: "Seeing as we are never going to communicate." She turns her back to me and strides away.

When I get home, I walk straight up to the cat's basket to pick him up. Katrin fed him in the morning and the wrapper from the medicine is still on the table. But he is lying there, dead, with his body stiff and his fur cold. My whole skin shrinks and I almost run back to work.

I have a meeting arranged with the Director. He is going to Stockholm at Easter, for a month, paid for by the Ministry for Education; would I please take over his administration while he will be away?

I tell him that the visiting lectureship is going well. I ask for more money for books, and whether we could set the exam later in the year—after all, I say, we can make up the rules how we want them now. He says that he will note my ideas. But he has already closed his notepad and started putting things away in drawers while I am still talking. I stay in my chair. He stands up. "Everything is fine?" he asks. I try to stand up too but my legs will not do it. And I try to say in a brisk, businesslike voice, "Oh yes, absolutely," but I cannot do that either. I say nothing at all for a few seconds, and then the words blurt out of my mouth.

"Actually, I have bad news. My cat is dead, I am just going home to bury it." But I do not want to. I do not know how to go about it, and I do not want to touch it. I have had that cat for six years. It turned up on my doorstep, very thin, and I took it in. It has slept on my bed and sometimes I talk to it. The vet cost more than my food for a month, just for one injection, but I did not begrudge it at all. Not at all! This is how I feel, but it was of course the wrong thing to have said to the Director: his brother died in a labour camp, two thirds of the way through twenty-five plus five.

He puts his hat on. There are plenty of cats, he says. You will get another one.

I pull myself together and think how there is a chance Katrin will get home before me, and perhaps she will wrap the cat up and deal with it. She's a practical person, and it would be easier for her since she has never loved it.

I took the afternoon off. I needed some groceries and I was walking up the main street when I saw the visiting lecturer on the other side. She had her hands stuck deep in her pockets, and that, I thought, is because she will keep leaving her gloves on the desk by the copier. One of the brass buttons with anchors on was missing from her coat. I wanted to turn and go away, but instead I froze, watching her peer into the shops. It seemed to me that she looked sad. Suddenly I knew what it must be like to be unable to speak or understand a word of the language that surrounds you, not even guess at it, to get everything half right or utterly wrong. It must be like walking around with a shell around you which no one can get through, hard outside but very, very tender beneath.

At that moment she saw me and crossed the street, shouting, "Piret! How are you!" even though it was only hours since she asked the same thing in the corridor, and even though we parted on a bad note. Again I found myself saying something unintended.

"You?" I asked. "How are you? You have not been lonely on your visit here, I hope?" She laughed. I burst into tears. She took hold of my arm.

"We'll go in here," she said. It was a new place, with a pink marble floor. All the crockery had a broad gold rim. The coffee was strong, and they served it with chocolate truffles on a saucer. In the middle of the ceiling hung a huge chandelier, a strange thing made from liqueur glasses and bits of welded kitchen implements and the chains from sink plugs: postmodernist, perhaps. I quite liked it.

"This is a very expensive place," I said, "for tourists only."

"Even so, let's have something else," she insisted. "Brandy, pastries, whatever. Look," she said, opening her wallet. "This is worth nothing at home. I'll have to put it in the airport charity box."

When everything was there on the table and the waitress had gone, she asked: "Are you going to say what was the matter out there?"

"No. It is not personal," I explained to her, "but here is a great space, where nothing can be said." She bit into a pastry, filling her mouth. She dusted her fingers, swallowed. She looked up and smiled lightly, as if none of the things that had taken place between us had ever been.

"These," she said, "are the best thing I've eaten since I came here. They remind me a bit of something I had in Greece, but those had mint in them too."

"We have the mint ones too," I found myself saying. "At Easter." Again, not something I intended, but the feeling was of it slipping, rather than jumping out, and not unpleasant.

"Do you? Does it grow here?" She patted her lips with a napkin. I wondered how old she was. Anywhere between thirty and forty, it was hard to tell. Like me, she had no wedding ring.

"I have two types of mint in my garden." I told her. "It dies and then comes up again, very reliable. Of course, you can dry it for winter." She took a lemon cake, I a cinnamon biscuit. "The biscuit!" I said. We laughed. I told her more about my garden: How I prepare the soil for carrots, and how I store them. I told her about the different kinds of daffodil bulb. Every now and then, between mouthfuls, she asked me to clarify: You have to put those under glass, I suppose? What time of year would that be? And I found myself thinking, These things are so easy to say!

The content, I sensed, is not the point at all. Yet at any minute, I knew, she might ask me something I didn't want to answer. At the same time, the feeling of waiting for this to happen was in some strange way almost a pleasure, and I was disappointed when finally the bill arrived without it having occurred. They brought our coats and only then, when we were buttoning them up, did she ask: "May we go back to your house?"

She did not at all mind burying the cat for me. The ground was still frozen, so it had to be a shallow hole. I watched from the kitchen window as she stamped the earth flat. Afterwards, we drank some wine, and then she returned to the flat in a taxi, which I paid for because she had spent all her money in the café.

Two days later, I saw her to her plane.

"Life goes on, Piret," she said. We embraced. I watched her through the passport control. "I'll write — " she called at the last minute.

The peonies were particularly good this year. The lettuce came in early. I have not replaced the cat, but I planted a new lilac close to where it is, yet not so close as to disturb it. Death is always such a shocking thing, making one reconsider life. And while once, here, that seemed endless, now it grows shorter all the time. I would like someone from outside to tell these things to. But it is July now, and no letter has come.

Johanna

I REMEMBER HOW WE GOT a cheap flight and spent almost a month in Spain, travelling on the buses and finding the cheapest places to stay. It was the first time Johanna had been abroad and she kept saying, "I could live like this." She was always pointing the colours out, the way the sky was like lavender, how perfectly it went with the cream and yellow and brown of the peeling paint, the purple flowers. I didn't really see it, but I liked that she was happy. "Even places that are dumps look okay here, don't they?" she said. When we visited the Alhambra, she cried because it was so beautiful, and that I could see: roses in the desert, the fountains and tiles. But mostly we were on the beaches. On some of them women could go topless, so she did, too. She tanned well. She had long brown hair that she put up in a knot when we went out at night.

But we had to go back home to Manchester. And there she was, knocked up. I remember talking about it in that galley kitchen of hers, facing each other across the few feet of lino, each of us with a countertop digging into our backs. I'd half moved into her place, but I still had my mother in Leeds to go back to if needs be. We were looking for work and meanwhile the social security was paying her rent. I had to move my stuff out when they visited, but it wasn't hard, just the one bag.

"Well, it's natural, part of life," I told her. "Happens. No need to make a big deal of it."

"So what are you saying?" she asked. She still had the sun-kissed look, but her face was tight.

"If you want it, have it," I said. "If you don't, don't. Simple as that."

"What I need to know," she said, "is, are you with me or not?"

"I am now," I said. "We get on well. I'm not going back to the Army."

"So what does that mean, Martin?" she asked. I felt myself pull away. I knew that I wasn't going to stay. I knew I didn't want the baby, or to be a father. A father! I didn't love Johanna, not the way it's meant or that she wanted. What I felt was a greedy, animal thing. I wanted the good times—and they were very good—and the thing with Johanna had been that she felt the same way, and until then there had been no more to it. But I didn't want to have a kid.

"Don't count on me," I said.

Even though I'd made myself clear, she decided to keep the baby. She couldn't stand the alternative, and at least Spain was a good starting point, she said, better than a quickie in some dank alley. She was sure it had happened in Granada. We hung on in a kind of limbo. She probably had hopes of me coming around, I that she'd lose it and we could go on how we were. When she went into labour I took her to the hospital. I did see the baby, but I was gone before she chose his name. You could earn good money in the building boom down south. I sent her cash, but I didn't go back. I spent the next decade on building sites, loved it. Moved on and up. Got my own business.

And another thing: by the time I met Johanna, it's possible I'd already had two other kids, depending on whether you could believe what those two women said. One in Germany and one in Cyprus. If she's doing it as a business, you expect her to take care of things. I never kept in touch in those cases, but I did try with Johanna. I kept clear of the boy—simpler that way—but I phoned her once in a while and for years I sent money, right until I realized how much she was drinking. At that point, I decided not to foot the bill and to stay out of it. By then the boy, Craig, she called him, was in his teens. I'd met Juliet. We married. I had my real kids, a house, the lot.

We moved a few times and so did Johanna, no doubt. I lost touch with her. God knows if she's even alive, now. And of course nowadays the doc tries to scare me, says to walk every day, eat my greens and cut out grease and salt. It's that time of life. I think of Johanna and the boy, Craig, wonder what happened to them, and suspect the worst: drugs, crime, an early grave. But if you don't actually know, there's hope, isn't there?

How do I feel about it, Juliet asked, and I must say, she took it well when I spilled the beans that night. *Feel*? Who I was back then wouldn't recognize who I am now. That was a different life and you can't turn back. I have my faults, but I pay our bills. I'll do anything for the girls, and I don't mess Juliet around. We went on a cruise this spring, just the two of us, with her sister looking after the girls. The house is detached, new roof, new windows, professional landscaping at the back, and I've got a full workshop so I can keep it all looking good. Once in a while I go fishing, switch off, stare at the water and the reeds. It's then that you start to think.

I've no photographs, nothing like that, but I remember Johanna. I remember her in the hotel room, where light through those old wooden shutters painted everything with stripes. She'd stretch out on the bed with a tooth mug of wine on the little table beside it. I remember her low laugh, the smell of her skin, how she tasted of the sea. I remember her standing in a huge, carved marble room in that palace on top of a hill. She smiled and cried at the same time, her head craned back to see it all. She comes into my head just as she was then. And sometimes I think, Suppose he, the boy, Craig, wants to find me, and I break out in a sweat, because the next thought after that is, Do I want him to?

Red Dog

EVERYONE AGREES THAT LAST summer Katie shelled the peas beautifully, though of course she was rather slow and lunch didn't happen until after two. It was a gorgeous day, the family all together for once. But why should time matter so much? Maria thought as they finally sat down at the table outside. Yet it does: the world rushes past like a train, going somewhere else and soon out of sight; it leaves people like Katie behind.

Katie is eight. Sometimes Maria thinks she notices a little improvement, but this could be wishful thinking: perhaps it's just that she, Maria, has got used to things, and how Katie is doesn't bother her so much anymore, and maybe that's the real improvement. How much does Katie remember? Maria asks herself. And what really goes on in there?

"You're coping so well," Malcolm says.

"Maybe it's easier, her not being my own."

"You could just as well say the opposite," he points out. They are truly doing their best, and they lose themselves in each other's eyes.

*

Summer's long gone. It's the middle of winter and Katie stands by the glass doors of the delicatessen. She can't read the green and gold writing but she can smell a rich sweetness that has an undertone of rotting in it, too, like laundry hampers, and she can see the whole cheeses and the jars of peaches and piles of sausages and the open boxes of chocolates in the window. Bottles, too, everywhere, stacked in pyramids, glittering.

She is to wait outside, because if she went inside she might knock something over: she gets too excited and shop assistants are very impatient at this time of year.

They won't be long. "Stay right here," Daddy said. "Don't move an inch." An inch is hardly at all...

Christmas music seeps into the street from the shops. There are no cars, but more people than she's ever seen. The windows glow and shine, everything is paintbox new and the air bristles with women's fragrances and spice. People in bright coats, singly, in groups, criss-cross the cobbled streets.

Opposite Katie, a machine turns in the window of the coffee shop, slowly browning beans. A bell rings each time the door opens or closes, and every time it does the smell of coffee rushes out and the ears of a dog tied to the sign that Katie can't read twitch and point. He is a medium-sized dog, mainly brown; he has a huge tail, dark blotches over his eyes, a crimson tongue. He sits sloppily on his haunches; his penis, half-erect, lolls between his legs. He fidgets, scratches, sees or smells something and stands, forgetting for a moment that he's tied. He tugs at the leash, stops, surprised. His tail points behind him like an arrow. Katie watches. She knows what he is. She learned the word months ago when someone's father bought one into Field House. Yesterday, they asked what she wanted for Christmas and she said it: Dog.

A couple leaves the coffee shop. The man is tall and thin and the woman is little and bright, with a shiny nose.

They stand for a moment, while the dog jumps and pulls and sniffs at them. They pat its head absently and they look at Katie, her puffy face and small eyes behind the enormous lenses, her straw-blonde hair in thin braids. She's wearing pink track bottoms and a puffy jacket in lime green. They shrug, unhitch the dog and walk away.

Katie badly wants to follow the man, the woman and the dog; she feels the tug of it but remembers how Daddy said *Don't move an inch*. She chews the woollen fingers of her gloves. She stamps her feet to keep them awake. She wants to turn and look in the shop window behind her, but if she does that, one thing will lead to another and she'll be inside before she knows it.

"Just look at all the people," Maria said. There are lots. Some of them have been past two or three times. Beyond the lights of the street, the sky goes violet, then black.

The dog returns, with the woman at the end of the lead. She tells the dog to sit but it doesn't: it sniffs Katie's shoes. The woman crouches down.

"Still here? Are you all right?" she asks. Her cheeks are pink and her eyes glitter with promise, like the lights in Christmas windows. "Only you were here last time we passed, over half an hour ago." An earring with feathers dances from one ear. Katie doesn't talk to strangers, but she nods. "Sure?" the woman says. "Is your mummy in that shop?" Her mummy lives in France now, and Maria is there instead, but Katie gives nothing away. She looks down at the dog. Breath pours from its mouth. Its brown eyes look back at her, slightly wicked. Its hot tongue slithers and quivers. The woman waits, still crouched down, while Katie strokes its head.

"He won't bite," she says. Katie feels the skull through the soft hair, the silky ears. She sinks both her hands into the rougher coat on the neck, buries her head there too. The smell is just how the dog looks. Dog. When she looks up, the woman breaks into a smile.

"Katie?" Maria calls from behind. The rest of them—Dad, Maria, Ben, Paul, Eliza—are waiting by the other door.

"Bye," Katie says into the dog's ear, and squeezes hard, forgetting the woman it belongs to, and hurries after her family. The dog's owner watches them: sees the tall man and the elegant woman, their many bags, the set of three ordinary children clustered around them, the fourth—something wrong with her—following several steps behind. Her shoulders are hunched up, her head hangs down. Normally, the woman thinks, with a kid that age, you'd have to keep an eye on her. But that one knows she's got to hang on to them, and they know she knows. She's following them, the woman thinks, shocked, the way a dog does.

Maria has a black coat with a fur collar and she smells of lipstick; Dad has an overcoat, Ben has a yellow anorak, Paul has a blue one, Eliza's is brown. They have been buying Christmas presents in Brighton, where everything glitters and somewhere is the sea: Katie remembers that. Pennies dance on it and balls bounce and sand gets in your mouth and the water draws a line wherever it touches you. In the summer you go to the sea. But in winter at Christmas you stay at home in the cottage—though the sea must still be there, waiting until next year? "Of course," Maria said. It doesn't go away, but it is cold and grey and all of the people on the beach have gone.

"Remember not to talk to strangers, Katie, love," Maria says as they climb into the new silver car.

"Dog," Katie replies.

"Please. But no, darling," Maria says. "We told you that yesterday."

Though, after all, there is a dog in one of her parcels, a small one with downwards-flopping ears. It's too smooth, it doesn't move; it isn't warm and it has no smell. Katie hits it over the back of a chair. And it doesn't yelp either, but Katie empties herself of the sounds of her disappointment and rage, pushes them out, her mouth an *O*, her eyes tight shut, her fists hammering. Now she must wait in the little room until she calms down. Maria rang Matron, who said that would be best.

"Otherwise we'll have to send you back, but we don't want to," Maria told her. Daddy, with the white beard stuck on, stood behind Maria and nodded to show he agreed.

There's a sofa in the small room, and a desk, and all the of bits of furniture and knick-knacks that don't fit in anywhere else. The window that looks out onto the big garden is wet, and the paint round it is mouldy because no one comes in here; it's so cold you can see your breath, but when the heat comes on the radiator smells like something sicked up.

Katie stands stone still in the little room while her heart runs away with her: It gallops. She clings on, just. It almost shakes her off. It bangs and bangs at her until it seems to fill her up and she wants to escape it, but it's inside her, the banging—not a noise you can hear, but a thing you can feel.

Ben calls from the other side of the door in his flat boy's voice: "Are you ready to come out, Katie? We don't like you being in there, but Dad says you must calm down."

Her heart runs even harder. There are footsteps, doors closing and she's alone again, which is better, and she looks out of the window at the brown, frosty grass. Then comes another knock, the door opening just a crack.

"Please understand," Maria says. "How could you have a proper dog, because who would look after it? But the toy dog is nice and you could tell him secrets and stories. Come on Katie, love, we want you to be with us, we're going to play games." Katie turns away. Her heart has paws; it trots on.

"Malcolm, it's our fault," she hears Maria say. "We shouldn't have asked her what she wanted. You should never—"

"We can only do our best," Daddy says. Then they've gone.

She can hear, distantly, the cries and shouts as they play the Christmas games. "Your family loves you very, very much," Matron said before Katie left, because she didn't want to leave, she never did. She felt safer at Field House. "You're very lucky to have somewhere to go for your summer holidays and for Christmas."

Perhaps it will be summer soon. Things are better in summer. Katie stands stock-still, just as she did when she was waiting outside the shop, and stares through the window. At the end of the garden is an old broken fence and then a field, just clods of chocolate-brown earth dappled with old stubble and crisped with frost. The sun is bright and low, everything underlined with shadow. Nothing moves. The sky beyond the garden is very blue.

And then an animal appears in the garden, big as a wish: a red dog. It freezes a moment, looking carefully in all directions. Nothing but its head moves. It pulls the cold air into a sharp muzzle, patched with white. Its brushy tail thrusts back after it, straight and still. Then it lowers itself to the ground and with a jerk twists on to its back, rubbing the back of its skull and its pointed ears on the ground. It stretches, rolls over, and for a moment it seems to look right at Katie. She takes a slow step closer to the window, and now the red dog stands on all four feet, facing towards the house. It gnaws briefly at its front leg, then turns and makes for the gap in the fence that leads to the field.

The window won't come open and Katie gives up because she doesn't want to lose sight of the red dog. It crosses the field, trots this way and then that, never in a straight line. Sometimes it disappears into the shadow patterns on the ground and then reappears somewhere else. She's pressed close to the window watching where it last was, when the door opens again.

Her heart is quite steady now.

"Hello, soldier," Daddy says. He has taken off the white beard. He holds out his hands. "Are you all right now?" he says. "Come play with us. We've really missed you." She nods, and follows him into the living room. He doesn't have to turn around and check that she is there.

"All over," he announces. "Ceasefire." It's very hot. There is a white plastic mat for the hands-and-feet game on the floor; balloons are stuck to the ceiling. Maria is lying on the sofa. Eliza and Paul are playing the game. Paul looks at Katie from underneath an armpit, his face red and upside down.

"You can join in next," he says. But Katie doesn't like the hands-and-feet game.

"Outside?" she asks, walking towards the picture window. Everyone falls silent. "It's cold, Katie, love," says Maria, holding out her arms.

"Coat—" Katie says. Everyone waits a minute, and then without saying anything Daddy fetches Katie her coat and her pink wellington boots. Everyone watches while he helps her put them on and then they open the sliding door for her.

"Don't go far!" they call, then close the door against the cold.

"She can't," Maria says. "That hedge on the back field has grown right over the top of the gate."

Katie runs around the side of the house to where she saw the red dog. She finds the place where it flattened the dry grass, and points herself the way it went. The red dog has a hot, deep smell. She'd know it anywhere.

"It really is getting better," Maria sighs. "We are getting the hang of this. Trial and error. Coping strategies." She sits up and takes a sip of sparkling wine. Malcolm squeezes her shoulder.

"I know it's not easy," he says, as Katie stumbles on up the hill, her face cold, her body warm, smelling the red dog—not knowing, yet, about the hedge.

Daddy

IT WAS HOT AND BRIGHT; we had to watch for poison ivy, for snakes. We were saving our water for when we arrived. My legs ached, and Daddy told me it was not much further, we were almost there. He held my hand. He caught me when my foot slipped. And he showed me where water burst out of the white rock, and then, just as suddenly, vanished, sucked into the ground. How come? Where did it go? Where we were walking was once a sea; the whitish rock beneath our feet was the remains of sea animals that lived before people ever were, and sank to the ocean floor when they died. This was calcite, which made limestone. Rainwater ate limestone slowly away. Vinegar would devour it overnight.

We watched dragonflies mate. The mother would lay eggs in the water and they would hatch into nymphs, which looked like beetles but had gills like a fish. They shed skins as they grew. At the same time, inside, they produced glittering wings, lungs, and enormous eyes. The nymph climbed out of the water, hung on a twig and split itself open. A dragonfly climbed out and dried its wings in the sun. Only the skin of the nymph remained, and Daddy found one for me, crisp and transparent. I looked hard, tried to make a picture of it in my mind.

I would change, too, as I grew up, but I did not have to ease myself out of a too-tight, wrong-shaped skin.

Suppose people did grow that way? Suppose we were just the beginning of something else? If you were trying to take off your skin, what would happen when you got to the hairy parts?

Good questions, Daddy said.

It was hot. We shared his last piece of gum and then he gave in, carried me until we reached a hole in the riverbank. Roots stuck out from the soil above it. We squeezed through. The cave was cool and smelled of mould; when my eyes adjusted I could see that it was big enough to be a child's room, though someone as tall as Daddy would not be able to stand up straight. We drank the water at last, and ate our apples. I put on my sweater and he strapped on the helmet with the flash-light attached. We were going to see something won-derful, he said, something I would remember all my life.

At the back of the cave was a low passageway which we entered on our hands and knees, I beneath him, as if we were animals. We were going downhill. His knees kept bumping into my feet; the rock bit into my knees. The floor of the tunnel was damp. My heart battered my chest.

Suppose, I asked, the lamp's battery ran out?

It would not, he said. But even if it did, bit by bit we would feel our way out backwards, and it would be all right.

Northern Lights

"LONDON," HIS CALLER IS SAYING. "I'm in London, by the road. In a phone box." She has a worn but once-rich voice, a faint accent he can't at first place.

"So what's the situation?" Joe adjusts his headset, ticks some boxes on the form. Opposite him, Paula is making one of her Blu Tack animals as she listens to her own call. She makes them every night: elephants, whales, a giraffe with a matchstick neck, even the occasional human being, naked and less than chaste—none of them bigger than the top digit of a thumb.

"I need somewhere to sleep," Joe's caller says.

"Can you tell me how come?"

"I'm forty years old and I've never had anywhere to damn well go," she says, "so how do I know how bloody-well come!"

"I'm sorry," he says, as they were taught, "but I need to ask these questions in order to help." There is no reply, just breathing.

"Date of birth: you must have been born in… '59?" he says.

"No," she says. "Fifth of May, 1935. It says so."

"You would be sixty-two, then," he says. There's a long pause. He expects her to argue, braces for it. But when she does eventually reply, her voice is small and disappointed, like something shrunk in the wash.

"I might be," she says. "I must be, then, mustn't I? I have to get back to Birmingham," she tells him, her voice still small, but firm.

"This is a London service. All I can try to do is get you a hostel place here," he says. "I can do that." *Vacancies: female 3, male 4,* the screen in front of him reads. He presses *next*. "Westminster," he says, "Southwark or—"

"Birmingham," she interrupts. "Birmingham, not somewhere else. It has Birmingham on my birth certificate. That's where I should be. Best all round. It's people not being in the right places that makes everything so hard, so very hard as they are, very hard and falling apart all the time, just violence and misery! If it's two thousand miles away or two miles away, same difference—it's no good, no damn good! Do you understand? The right place stops you breaking up in bits. People should go to there, wherever it is. You must know that. If you don't, you're in the wrong, fucking, damn place yourself." She's breathing hard.

"When were you last in Birmingham?"

"I remember—" she says brightly, "it had a green door."

"Can you remember the road name?"

"No," she says. Then: "Yes! *Gallstone Drive*. I think it was thirty-six or sixty-six. Call them. They know me there. Tell them Laura."

"I'll put you on hold, Laura," he says. "Gallstone Drive," he hisses at Paula, who is taking a call at the desk opposite, and enjoys seeing her try to keep a straight face. He calls emergency social services in Birmingham. *Gallstone Drive!* But there is a place she might mean, the woman there says: a number thirteen Galveston Road is her best suggestion. It's what used to be called a "home."

"Might be the place," Laura says, anxious. "Ask about the green door."

"Laura? Oh, you mean Mary Coates," says Alec at Galveston Road. Yes, they certainly do remember her. And perhaps they could take her back, though he will have to ask the relief manager who is currently sorting out a dispute in the television room. "I'll be right back to you, mate," he says.

"I don't want to raise your hopes too much," Joe tells Laura, or Mary, "but hang on there. I've spoken to a bloke called Alec; he does know you. I'm on the case."

"I've got to pee!" she says. "Can't wait all night." The line goes dead. Immediately Alec-at-the-home comes on the other one and says *yes*. Get her up there and they will take her. Unfortunately, Joe explains, he may have lost her. But just in case, he makes all the arrangements—overnight here, travel grant in the morning. Then he takes several routine calls. Another hour passes; it is nearly ten.

"After all that, the Gallstone woman vanished, would you believe," he tells Paula, whose turn it is to take the phone home and run the service through the night. "Maybe she'll call later," he says. "I'll give you all the details."

"I hope she doesn't. I hope it's quiet. I feel like death warmed up," Paula says, then sees the expression on his face. "Oh, Joe, you just lose some," she says, stretching her arms above her head and pushing her chair back.

They turn off the computers, remove their headsets. He watches Paula pluck her Blu Tack animals one by one from the top of the screen, squeeze them into a blob and put that in the top right desk drawer. She has always refused to explain why she does this.

"Look!" she says, pointing. The red light flashes and it is Mary, Laura, whatever her damn name is.

"Hello?" she says. "It's me."

Joe has handed his car over to his daughter Lucy so Paula gives him a lift as far as the bus stop.

"I'm thinking of having streaks and one of those urchin cuts. What do you think?" she says as they get into the car, an old Saab. There's a plastic dinosaur glued to the dashboard, a litter of tissues and wrappers everywhere else. "You must be so excited, Joe!" she says as they pull out into the main road. "Most people still live in the same sort of place all their lives, don't they? There's a leaving party next week," she glances quickly his way, "but I can't come. So I'll say it now, I might as well: you'll be missed, Joe. You—you're a lovely man, you know. Now don't say anything or I'll bloody well cry." She gasps. The car swerves and then she rights it.

"Look, shall we stop a bit?"

"No!" she snaps. He's not sure what's going on.

"I will miss you too," he says. "And the job." Though it's not a job, as such, just something he began after a bad patch, so as to keep himself plugged into the world. Helping others worse off than yourself, etc.

She nods silently, her lips pursed, heaves in another breath, says: "Well here it is—you might as well know now that I've always felt—that I have a bit of a crush on you. To put it mildly." She speaks in a brittle monotone, staring hard at the taillights in front of us. Now tears creep down her cheeks.

"Paula!" he says. "I had no idea! I really enjoy your company. But you know—"

"Oh, sure, sure, sure," she says. "That's why only now." She is so much younger than him. Of course, it is flattering. It also is shocking, to think of her feeling like that. To think of those times he has moaned to her about Christina and that she has just sat there and said nothing. He has always liked Paula, her quirkiness, busy fingers, quick smiles and sudden, absolute hard-headedness, but he's never thought of fancying her, and it dawns on him only now that he could: her face is plump, her body small and tightly round. What might those fingers do with warm, living skin? But she's right, there is nothing much to be said on the subject now, because he and Christina are moving just about as far away as you can get. An opportunity too good to turn down. A bit of an adventure. A crazy thing.

Just about a year ago, he sat at the kitchen table, thinking of nothing much. It was hot; he was wearing shorts. Christina came up behind him and put her hands on his shoulders, then bent over and kissed the top of his head. He smelled her warm skin and her light perfume, her breath and the whiff of other people's smoke that clung to her clothes. She slipped her hands down, over his chest and belly, left them there, rested her chin on his shoulder. Joe, she said, I think you'll like my news.

Or else you could say it has happened incredibly slowly, that it began twenty-five years ago, when they decided to marry. They'd been together all through her endless college years. He liked to look, she to talk. He was her relief, she his stimulus: they were opposites, but agreed on which people and books they liked, on politics (more or less), on the fact that whatever they were supposed to be, the reality was that she was driven and he was unambitious. It was harder to agree about where they should live.

Joe wanted to be in the country, and not just ordinary, agricultural country. He wanted a wild, open place, or as close to one as possible. He wanted to paint big abstracts, maybe branch into sculpture, and at the same time make some money by fixing a barn into a cottage, or running a guest house. He'd hill-walk, take Christina's clothes off, make love, eat, sleep.

She was for the city: she had her doctorate and was going to make her way. Well, she'd be the one to make regular money and he had to agree that it was only the hill-walking that a city really ruled out, and besides, the holidays... They moved, city to city: York, Sheffield, Leeds, and finally London. More of a city each time, but always a garden. Two kids, Ben and Andrea, him doing the lion's share. When Joe still used to smoke, at night he would sometimes sit for half an hour or so in the garden before he went to Christina in bed. He could feel the night flowing around him then and see stars; that was at least part of what he had meant by living somewhere wild.

Looking after the kids gave him a certain distinction with the various neighbours, and a definite curiosity value with her academic friends. He still sketched, but the painting got lost. Well, he would joke, he used to paint Christina, but now he never saw her. She wrote her books—about sugar, slavery, tobacco, rubber, chocolate—and that meant travelling.

He met lots of other women as he carted Ben and Andy around. He had an afternoon-sex phase. A whisky-drinking phase. Depression, which eventually led to the job on the nightline. For a while, in the middle of all this, he understood that Christina was ashamed of him. At one point, she moved another man into the house, a small, bearded semiotician from Hamburg, but Joe stayed drunkenly put, and Gustav eventually departed. And then, suddenly, somehow, their friends were divorcing and amazed at them for being still together. "Home-husbands" became briefly fashionable and they were pioneers. Ben left home, then Andrea. They had done the whole thing.

"What news?" he asked Christina, idly, that warm night almost a year ago, though, truth be told, he wanted her at the moment far more than he wanted to know whatever-it-was. She was one of those fine-boned women who get sparer and more polished with time, and more energetic. She was flexible, held herself like a girl. Whereas he was a soft man, plump, sprawling, his hair thinning in the middle. More than ever, he wanted to draw her, to follow those lines through.

"I've got an interview for what looks like a fantastic post in Canada," she whispered in his ear. "Very low teaching load. And listen, this is the point: it's a wild place. There are wolves and bears. Elk, lynxes. Hardly any people. Harsh winters. Come in the other room, I'll show you."

They sat either side of the fireplace, which, when they first moved in, he'd knelt at for two days, stripping off its layered paint. In deference to Joe's dislike of electric light, especially at dusk, they sat there in a kind, soft dimness. Christina spread out brochures, photographs and a map. He could fly out with her; they could spend a week or so, see the place. She leaned against him and told him how she sometimes thought he must feel he'd had something perfectly decent in life, but not what he set out wanting.

"You've done so much for me," she told him, taking his hands in hers. "Made everything possible. I do know that. And maybe this is a chance for us both to get what we want, for us both to be satisfied together. Maybe you'd start painting again, here. Look." Joe looked at the pictures. The daytime skies were a very pure blue, the ice on the lake luminous. In one nighttime image, snow covered the ground and a kind of green curtain rippled across the night sky: the northern lights.

It was very quiet in their living room and Christina's bright voice grew unusually soft. "I love you," she said.

He felt a tender queasiness in his stomach, to do with being loved by Christina, and told also to do with the idea of painting again. He could see how that might happen, over there.

A new life. A fairy tale. And indeed, among the photographs she had brought to show him, the couple who had preceded them, wearing puffy jackets trimmed with fur, skied across a frozen lake towards a wooden house backed by snow-laden trees. He did not ask: When did you apply for this?

They flew out. The city's mills belched smoke and steam into the clear sky but the university was half an hour away, a brand new campus in the middle of forest and mountains, small but well-resourced, friendly and interesting. They kayaked on the lake they had seen in the photographs and watched eagles hunt for fish. You could live right there, on the edge of the water, walk out to it, swim. She was offered the job.

"You're going," Paula says in the car, "halfway around the world!"

"That's the plan," he says.

When she pulls in at his bus stop, they say goodbye and kiss cheeks awkwardly. They'll keep in touch, of course. Email and so on.

"Enjoy your new life!" she says through the open window, and she seems quite okay now, completely back to normal. "Make Christina do some of the packing!" she tells him as she prepares to pull away. People have always made remarks like this, as if he has to be defended from his own wife. Given the situation, he lets it pass, just waves.

What does he think of this crush of Paula's? Would he? Probably not, now, but in some obscure way it feels like some kind of reward for the years out in the cold. What else in his life has he not been aware of? Are things going to open up, like some extraordinary rose? From now on will it all be different?

The bus lurches into view, and he sits opposite a man he encountered once when he was photocopying for Christina at the garage: a small, stocky man wearing army surplus gear, very tanned, with a grizzle of grey-blonde hair and bright blue eyes. He has a faded canvas haversack on his lap. The last time they met, this man told Joe he was just about to buy some property in, of all places, South Africa: a wonderful bungalow with acres of fruit trees and flowers going for less than a beat-up flat would cost over here.

"Whites are leaving," he'd said, "scared, but it'll blow over in the end. Everything does, and that country has it all. Look around you, mate," he said. "Used to be better. I've got a one bedroom and a balcony, but I'd rather have acres in the sun and someone bringing me a cocktail on a frigging tray, now wouldn't you?"

Joe agreed, for the sake of oiling the wheels. He thought how Christina would be giving the man what-for. He opened the copier to free a stuck sheet.

"Machines," the man said, "copiers, calculators, computers, phones, cars: it adds up to you can't do something you used to be able to do. I make sure I know how to fix anything I buy. I add up my grocery bill, do a crossword every day. I cook my own food. In any situation, I ask how could I cope if things went wrong? How would I get out of here if there was a fire? A power cut? If civil war broke out, what would I eat? I make sure I know." He jabbed his finger at his own chest. "I'm a survivor." His eyes burned, intent, but then he'd broken into a boyish smile and offered his hand to shake. Now he sits on the bus, face loose, eyes distant, and when Joe meets his eyes, there's no recognition. So, Joe thinks as he gets off at the corner, you haven't gone yet. But I will.

It's fully dark now, the streetlights pooling on the pavement. He walks the few hundred yards home, passing a blowsy girl waiting for a different bus and the hunched, grey-haired man who always seems to be at the corner of their street, smoking and watching his terrier defecate in the gutter. Joe passes him with a nod, walks on, taking in the gardens—one wildly fertile, a miniature jungle, the dark shapes of bushes and plants bursting out of the small space. Its owner, often seen wearing a blue checked housecoat to water and trim, is sitting inside with the curtains open and the TV on. Another patch is paved in stone, with just one large pot containing a eucalyptus tree to one side of the door, a galvanized watering can at the other. He has never seen the person it belongs to but they have a piano and play like a god, though it's unpredictable—sometimes he catches it for several days on end, then not at all for months… How many thousand times has he seen, smelled and heard all this, this typical semi-suburban London street with trees and Victorian houses, this place where people come to bring up kids and not be totally broke? Why is it still so interesting?

At the gate to their house, he stops, listens to the distant purr of the traffic on the main road. A telephone rings, a light is turned off, a breath of wind runs through the plane trees. The next-door neighbour (and there's another story) puts a bottle on the step, a particular, hollow, chinking sound which makes Joe know he will miss doing so himself, and that he will also miss the milkman, Dave, an extraordinary fellow with a passion for Dostoyevsky who says he was once was a priest and, after his shifts, goes home to work on a movie script that will knock the world flat. And he will miss Carol, two streets away in the estate, who stops by or calls once a week or so to share what further sense she's made of her mess of a life. She's in her seventies. He met her during his drinking phase; she's still in hers.

"Are you there?" she'll say. "It's this: there is no Continuity." Or, "I'm pretty sure that there is no Essential Self. Most people can fool themselves, but because of the life I've lived, I can't." Or, "There's only Memory, dear. I'm hanging on to mine by the skin of my teeth." She hasn't called so often lately, and he realizes, as he thinks of her, that this could well be because he's going. In two weeks' time. They have a leaving party planned.

He walks slowly up the path and lets himself into the house. Christina is in the kitchen, talking on the phone to her mother in Scotland. She's wearing just a tee-shirt, no underwear. Out of habit he stares at the gap between her legs, at the top.

"Please don't worry," she's saying. "Nothing permanent. We've made absolutely no long-term decisions. We're thinking five years or so, then think it over. Like I said, just renting out the house. Who knows what will happen. You'll come out to visit us—think of that! And we'll be back for holidays. We'll come once a year and stay twice as long." She makes a face. Christ-my-mother! it says, but Joe doesn't raise his eyes in sympathy as he usually would.

They're letting the place unfurnished and shipping out about half of their things: that's already gone. The rest goes into storage at the end of the week. He walks through to the garden to bring in the washing he put out earlier, but she has already done it. So he sits on the bench instead and he remembers the smile spreading across Christina's face when he told her yes, they would go to Canada. How it melted him, then. Yet in memory, now, he finds something he doesn't quite like about that smile, a shiftiness, a split second's barely concealed amazement, as if she had got away with something. Her voice seeps into the garden.

"Oh—but they're thrilled to have us out of their hair!" she's saying, in the kitchen. "You know what it's like at that age. So busy with their own lives. Ben is almost certain to be working in the States. Andrea's going to be doing her Ph.D. in Germany..."

He comes in again, passes her without looking, slowly climbs the stairs. He sits on the temporary double bed and looks out at next door's garden, faintly lit from their living room window. Sometimes he sees foxes there.

He imagines calling Carol. She certainly owes it to him. Carol, he'd say, it's this, and there'd be the click of her lighter, her first suck of smoke: Go on then, dear, I'm all ears.

Christina is standing in the doorway.

"Don't put on the light," he says.

"What's up?" She runs her fingers through her newly cut hair. "Hey, you've not done a great deal of tidying up today. And that blind needs fixing. Still, I dare say we'll get through most of it on the weekend. Andy's coming to help. I met her for lunch, along with a strange friend with a stud in his lip."

"I feel as if I don't want to go," he says, and she laughs.

Then she asks: "Why?"

"I love it here," he says.

"You'll love it there too, you know. That's how you are, you know you are." She comes into the room and picks up one of his socks from the floor by the bed, drops it into a drawer, then comes over and crouches at his feet. Outside, the sky is thickest ink—a wonderful mix of indigo and black, and, in a diffuse but final way, he knows that something has been disturbing him ever since Christina first mentioned the move. A question.

"Supposing I've changed my mind, suppose I want to stay here," he begins, "would you still want to go, for yourself?" His head clears, as if from years of fog. His body settles firm around his bones. He fixes her face, studies it, looking for clues.

"I have resigned, Joe," she says. Not what he asked.

"They'd have you back."

"Not this year! What is this? Talk about appalling timing," she says, and she's absolutely right. "This is what you always wanted," she says and, again, she's absolutely right, but his heart pounds and his voice rings out.

"Answer me, please—would you still want to go? Is this for you or me? Sorry," he adds more quietly.

"It is an incredible chance, Joe," she says, "Not just my job. For a new life."

But, Joe is thinking, I want the one I have! I want to know what Paula looks like with her new haircut. Whether Dave ever writes his screenplay, or Mary Coates got to Birmingham... The place where he lives surrounds him. It's a raft—solid, well made—and if he clings to it, it will protect him from Christina's plans, from his own acquiescence, from anything.

"I'm sick of being jerked about," he says.

"We've been here nearly ten years!"

"If you're doing it for me, I don't want to go, okay? I don't want to go. I hope that's clear. Are you doing it for me, or for you with me on the side? That's my question—so answer it, will you, please!"

She turns on the light by the bed. They face each other, just a few secrets each between them. Her eyes are bright, the skin around them ever so slightly creped. "I want to stay here. Us to stay here," he says, sitting there on the bed with his thinning hair and soft belly, his unpainted pictures, the empty house all around. He's desperate for a drink he mustn't allow himself.

"Just when I've made it work out, in the end!" she says. Her voice tears at its edges—at him too—but the fact is, she still has not told him: Is she doing it for him, or for her, with him on the side? He has never been so angry, not in his entire life. It's a massive charge, running through him, like a kind of electrocution. He could burn up, strike out—but then it hits him that after all this time, she and he are still the same as they ever were, only more so.

Everything dissipates. Her face is just a blur. Her clothes sigh as she moves towards him. Outside, it's very dark.

"Joe?" she asks, "Joe, why cry now?"

Open Water

MITCH HAS BEEN WAITING all week for Tara to get back to him. Only when in the water is he separated from his phone. It's lucky, he thinks, as he punches in the code to disable the alarm and lets himself in, that he has to be here. The pool rested overnight, and now lies smooth, ready to give him a break, to take him elsewhere, as it always has. Outdoor, indoor, underground, rooftop, exclusive, inclusive, filthy, sparkly-clean, Olympic, 25-metre, salt-water, UV—any pool will do. Mitch has his favourites, but Fourth Street, with its banner—"Home of the Sharks"—is the one he thinks of as his. Twenty-five metres, eight lanes, three metres at the deep end, it's housed in an aging and never-splendid building, yet still seduces him with that turquoise glow, with those threads of reflected light knitting and releasing themselves in a dance that is both loose and contained. The pool promises buoyancy and escape; it taints the air with a tang of chlorine (fainter these days, due to the UV) to which he has no objection at all.

He pulls off his sweatshirt, dumps his backpack on the floor, and pushes through the door at the back of reception onto the deck. The air is warm and moist. Condensation gathers on the picture windows that look out into the woods. The hum of the ventilation and mechanical systems seems oddly loud when the pool is empty, but it is always there, lurking deep beneath the shouts and splashes that bounce themselves to mush between the water and the walls and mount to a crescendo at about four in the afternoon. It is a kind of silence that you only hear if you're there first or last thing, when the swimmers have gone and the water is, as now, very nearly still, waiting for a dive to break its surface, for the dive which will connect Mitch to all his other dives, and to all the waters of the world.

For a racing dive, you climb on the blocks, which angle towards the water, one leg at the back, one at the front. You keep your back straight, offer your chest and the heart beating steadily inside it to the water. Waiting, you push with your legs and you pull back with your arms so that when the light flashes and the buzzer sounds, you spring forward with doubled force. Your arms come back to your sides, but right away you bring them up so that they point your way in. You hyper-extend, tense your core and extend your legs so that once your fingers part the surface, you slice into the water and enter it without wasting any of the power you put into the spring. You're looking for horizontal distance. On the other hand, diving for diving's sake from a platform or a springboard depends on the takeoff but is all about the flight and the entry. Straight, pike, tuck, free: it is, when you get down to it, mainly about being in the air, and that has never interested Mitch.

The water closes behind him. He kicks hard, stays under for three quarters of a length before he surfaces, ready to start the routine that will set him up for the day: Practise what you preach. Swim the swim. Well, Mitch likes what he does. Whatever happens with Tara, he'll hang on to that.

"And whatever she says, you are going to have to be fine with it," Annette told him last night, when he couldn't sleep and tried to slip out of bed without waking her. They sat up and talked in the dark.

"Yes," he said, "but still..." He stared straight ahead, out of the window, picking out the shapes of the garden trees he'd planted, but he could feel Annette studying at his face. Beneath the sheets, she put her hand on his leg.

"And either way, it's just good she agreed to think it over."

"I know."

"And it will be fine for Tara, whatever she chooses to do." Annette took her hand from his leg, touched his face, made him look at her. She pulled him into a kiss, offered her body for him to forget himself in. Afterwards, he plunged into oblivion and did not wake until the alarm sounded at five. Her side of the bed was empty, and he found her hunched over her tea in the kitchen downstairs, looking every bit of her age. Five-oh! More importantly, five years older than him, which, these days, she could not forget, whereas, left to himself, he would. A decade ago, when he was thirty-five, the gap had seemed like nothing at all. In five years' time it would be that way again, or even something to celebrate: if the years were laps or miles, you'd be proud of them, for heaven's sake! But the thing is, they've not had kids of their own. They met a bit too late for that.

"So then *I* started worrying," Annette said, "but not about Tara. One way or another, Mitch, she'll be okay."

"*Don't* worry," Mitch told her. "I promise you, the last thing I want to do is drink."

"I didn't mean that," Annette said. She was worrying about the potential impact on their relationship. It was all connected, she said.

"Please. Just *don't*," he said. Running late, he squeezed her shoulder and hurried to the car.

He'd been with Annette for about a year—they had just bought the house—when Tara first showed up on a late Friday afternoon. He was teaching a shared lesson and noticed a family come on the deck. The mother, skinny, had thick blonde hair and a pierced belly button; the man stood very tall and fit. A tattooed dragon coiled up his arm. The girl, Mitch put at about seven, and they'd dressed her in a turquoise bikini—Why, he asked Annette later, do people do that? He watched as the mother, showing off her own figure in a similar suit, crouched down, felt the water, mock-shivered, stood again. For a moment, all three of them waited in a line at the shallow end, considering the expanse of water ahead of them. Then the little one threw herself in—not exactly a dive, and perhaps the lifeguards weren't looking, or else they let it go. She surfaced, gulped some air and hurtled towards the deep end, her hands smashing into the water, but fast—and, the thing was, it looked messy as all hell, but she pretty much had the stroke: face in, the arm's reach coming right from the hip, the twist of the neck, the timing. It was all there, ready, and Mitch just had to stop and watch.

He didn't know it then, but nature versus nurture was a topic he and Tara's mother would, in the coming years, return to many times. Of course, he'd tell her, you need to train. But some people start from a better place. Height is good; long limbs and big hands and feet are a tremendous asset (look at Mr. Phillips, now!), and some (not necessarily the same ones) just have a better constitution and a more efficient metabolism than others. To some extent, the lack of any of these assets can be overcome with hard work and the right mindset. But an understanding of how to move in water—*feeling* the physics, not knowing it—that's probably innate, and, he'd tell her, that feeling is worth more than anything and it is the very best place to begin. That's what he'd say, and certainly it seemed to him as he stood waist deep, watching, that this girl had more than begun. She was halfway up the pool before her mother jumped in after her, breaststroking along with her head up, arms and legs out of synch, fighting her own efforts every inch of the way.

"Tara," she shouted, "wait! You've got to be able to stand!" Forget that, Mitch thought, as Tara closed in on the end rail, slowing down a bit, but not much. She was pushing it—another thing not everyone wants or is able to do. The two boys in the water with him, for example, were time-wasters, reluctant to go a hair's breadth out of their comfort zone, and therefore doomed to progress at a glacial pace, but there were ten minutes of the lesson left so he turned his back on Tara and returned to the drill for the dolphin kick.

"That kid could go a long way, very fast," he told Annette in the evening. "Could be a great swimmer. I'm absolutely sure of it. And I could help. I feel like I *should*. It's weird. I've not felt like this before."

After the lesson, he dried off and pulled on his "Coach" tee-shirt for maximum professional effect. The new family were back in the shallows, and he went right over and squatted down.

"That's some awesome swimming you do," he said to Tara, then looked at her parents. "Who taught you, your dad?" The man with the tattoo laughed.

"Afraid not, " he said. "You're looking at the world's worst."

"Her cousin taught her in the lake," the mother said.

"You're a bit of a fish," Mitch told Tara. "How old are you?"

"Seven and a half," she said. She was looking right at him, had been ever since he came over. It was clear to Mitch that she very much wanted to hear what he had to say.

"One thing—" he told her, "try keeping your hands like this, and sliding them in forward without a splash, then you can pull more water...see? Angle them like this. It should feel like you're pulling and the water's pushing back. But don't quite close up your fingers. Like so. You'll catch more water. Feel it? That's the way." He turned back to the mother.

"You know, she might enjoy our swim team." He kept his tone light, even though he had a very serious feeling about it.

"We're not really joiners," she said, and looked away. There was no point in being pushy, and, as he explained to Annette, it was all too easy for parents to think you were some kind of pervert, especially once your hair started to thin. These days, he said, it's probably better all round to be female, but some things can't be helped. Thank god, Annette said. So Mitch didn't ask whether they were passing through or new to the area, or where the kid went to school. He just grinned and backed off.

"Mitchell McAllister," he told them as he stood up. "Here most mornings, afternoons, and evenings. Enjoy the pool."

"It's freezing!" Tara's mother said. They did keep the water cool. That was what swimmers needed. Management appreciated the needs of the club, plus those few degrees saved a fair bit.

"Oh, it's not so bad," he told her, smiling. "You'll soon warm up."

"Maybe I'll never see them again," he told Annette.

Back then, the house took up all their free time. That night they were painting the lounge in Ivory and Arctic Moss. He was on the ladder, she was cutting in by the baseboard. They each craned their necks to look at the other.

"Well," she said, "let's see how it goes," and there was a feeling that they had agreed to something, though neither of them knew exactly what.

A week or two after their first meeting, he ran into Tara's mother in the lobby. Her hair was wet, and she had a rolled-up towel under her arm; a nice woman, he thought, but a little too thin and too intense, her eyes shiny-bright, the angles and planes of her face more like sculpture than flesh. He was just arriving, she was on her way out.

"Hey, Mitch, right?" she called out. "We chatted the other week. Tara pestered me to bring her back so she can show you her new arms. She's been practising in the air."

"Cool!" he said, feeling his heart rate pick up: excitement, self-justification, hope—a cocktail of many things.

"Well," she shrugged, "it's a half-hour drive, and we have a lot to look after right now. Fencing the yard, keeping the darn chickens alive, re-plumbing up the house. We just can't make too many trips. And I'm not a fan of your freezing water! So finally we made it—and then we missed you. Sabrina, by the way." She offered her hand.

"I start later on Tuesday and Thursday afternoons," Mitch explained as Tara emerged with her dad from the family change-room. Jason: Mitch shook his hand, too. It was cold still from the pool.

"Scoot back in, I'll watch you now," he told Tara. The parents looked at each other.

"You two stay dry," he told them. "Get a coffee, tell Chris it's on me. Five minutes, okay?"

She jumped right in, looked up at him. She was waiting for his say-so, but at the same time, he had a feeling she was in charge. *Okay,* he thought, *I'm yours.*

"Up to the end and back," he told her, "but remember, it's not a race. I want what's called *good form*. I'll walk up on the side here and I want to see you make your hands go in perfectly and pull back the water just as I told you, every single time." At the end, she was breathing hard, which told him she had tried for speed *and* form, and that her endurance needed work. But the hands *were* perfect, and her eyes sought his: *How was that? What did you see? What next? Show me!* They were blue-grey eyes, big, the same as her mother's, but her gaze was untroubled and they picked up some of the colour of the water. She was all about what came next, about being in the water, about wanting something from him and wanting even more from herself.

"Attagirl," he beamed back at her. "You got it. Next time I'll show you the flip turn." He picked her out a decent pair of goggles from the lost and found and told her to ask her parents to get her a one-piece and book her in for a free trial lesson: that way, they wouldn't have to get wet themselves.

There was another long gap and then, over the course of a six-week set, Tara learned her dive and turn, and the beginnings of a pretty decent fly. They started on her dive.

"It's like I'm giving her what she's wanted all her life," he told Annette. "Amazing. Totally committed. But she needs to be part of something."

Maybe she needs other kids to swim with, was how he would put it to Sabrina.

"If your folks do say yes, at this time of year you'd practise every day before school and the dry-land training Tuesday and Thursday after school. Meets, that's the races, are every month or so until the real season starts and you don't have to come to every single one. Later it gets to be a little bit more. But we do take August off. You need talk it over with your mom and dad." Take a deep breath, he told himself. Submerge…hold it. Let it out very slowly. Wait.

Depth is about the water pushing in on you and separating you from the familiar world. Some of those drawn to go deep want none of the careful calculation of pressure and gases, the attention to time and meticulous checking of equipment that scuba entails; they prefer to extend their innate physical capacities as far as possible and dive free of equipment, with just a lungful of air to sustain them and a dangling rope to help them find their way back up. A free-diver learns his or her body as if it were both friend and enemy: how deep it will willingly go, how to push it further, how to increase lung capacity and oxygen absorption, how to slow the heartbeat and move without wasted effort; to evaluate, accept and transcend pain.

Mitch once witnessed a free-diving record. He was on the crew of the *Shirley*, waiting for Herman Fischmann (could you make up a name like that?) to surface. He held his own breath in sympathy, but managed only two minutes. He burst into tears when the bloke's shaven head emerged—it was like seeing a baby born—and on top of that he felt a kind of water-man kinship, though personally he was not especially drawn to depth. For him, it's speed, economy and distance, not depth, not so much. But he certainly understood the dedication involved.

He knew that Sabrina and Jason did not quite get where—who—Tara was, but he had high hopes that they would.

"If you think about it, what I ask of these kids is no different from, say, learning the piano," he told Annette. They had the new kitchen in by then—granite, gas stove, the lot—and made a point of using it.

"Hmm... You don't have to play piano at six thirty, travel half an hour to get to it and pack your breakfast," she said, which was fair enough.

Annette owned Valley Fitness, the gym in town. She had it first with her ex, then on her own; she was hoping to sell it before too long. She was a keep-fitter, not an athlete, but she understood training and competition.

"I'm not strict," he continued. "Intrinsic motivation is where I come from, not carrots and sticks. After a year, I expect a little more, and so on. And she'd lift the whole team: it's not just about the obvious athletes. Some kids are signed up to get a bit of exercise, others for the friendships, but then once they are in, it changes, and some of them suddenly take off. They all get something out of it. But with Tara, I have to tell you, I'm thinking the Nationals in a few years and then looking right ahead to the Olympics in 2016."

"That's an awful long way to look," Annette said. "What about here and now? Could we forget Tara for an hour or so?" He grinned back at her and complimented her on the salmon she had cooked, tried to bring his mind back to the two of them and the here and now, but the truth was, he could not forget: even when he did not think of Tara, she was there, waiting in the back of his mind. And before long it got to the point where both he and Annette dreamed about Tara, her times, her moments of victory, but also things like injuries, forgetting her suit, losing her goggles, or beginning to struggle for her breath. Many times, in his sleep, he dived in and rescued her.

You must do whatever the lifeguard says, Mitch always tells his swimmers, and use your common sense: don't swim alone. Remember that water, however much you love it, does not love you back. It simply does what it must do according to the laws of physics and the conditions at the time, and while it is essential to life, it can also end it, and swiftly, too. Humans are not amphibious. *How can you tell if someone is drowning?* he asks. Hardly anyone has ever had the right answer: swimmers in distress splash and shout, but drowning itself is silent and swift. There's just not enough air to make any noise. The head goes back, the arms spread out and push down on the water until, for a moment or two, the mouth breaks free of the surface, exhales, gasps—but then it goes under again. With each surfacing the inhalation is smaller, the amount of carbon dioxide in the blood greater, the arms weaker, and in a minute or less it's impossible to surface at all; water is inhaled and the larynx constricts, sealing the air tube to protect the lungs. The brain, starved of oxygen by now, soon shuts down—though the victim may still be resuscitated, if pulled out of the water and treated before cardiac arrest occurs.

In order to flush the carbon dioxide from their lungs and so delay the breathing reflex triggered by its build-up, some swimmers hyperventilate before a distance or depth dive. It's a high-risk strategy, since the diver may black out due to oxygen deprivation before they feel the urge to breathe. Typically, these drowned divers are found, too late, on the bottom of the pool. So, no panting and gasping before you dive in, he tells his swimmers, and no breath-holding contests. I know what I'm talking about, believe me. And even though you are going to be excellent swimmers, please wear your flotation devices when you row across the lake or go sailing with your uncle. Suppose the boom swings and knocks you unconscious before you fall in? And by wear, I mean buckle it up.

Sabrina and Jason's overgrown acreage and 1910 farmhouse with authentic shingles came cheap, but they had to install fences and drains, fell trees, extract rocks from the soil, and then plant five hundred grape vines and two hundred lavender bushes, all at the same time as trying to run a web design business, grow their own ultra-healthy food—including chickens—without using chemicals, and raise a family. Eventually they would be showing visitors round on tours and tastings as well, and Sabrina would be making and marketing organic lavender products: oil, hand cream, soap and such. *Big dreams and laudable aims*, was how Mitch put it to himself. You never knew how things would turn out, but it sounded to him like a miserable amount of work, unless you had money behind you.

"Nice property," he said when they showed him and Annette around.

"I wish you hadn't put this team idea in her head," Sabrina said. "All that time spent on one thing, especially at this age, seems crazy! The reason we chose home-schooling was to avoid competitiveness and peer pressure and have her enjoy her childhood."

"Well, yes," Mitch said, and met the eyes fixed on his face, the mottled grey irises darkly ringed and suspended in blue-tinged white. His feeling was that Sabrina desperately wanted to do the right thing, but had no instinct for what it was. Part of her knew this, but another part, the part mainly in charge, did not.

"There is all that," he said. "And it would be a big commitment. And you're her mom, so you know best. The club is competitive, but it's not *just* about competition. It's very sociable. They work hard and they have a lot of fun together—that might be a big plus if she's mainly with you guys. And some people just naturally like to strive. Look at it this way: she's competing against herself right now. It might be healthier to let her do it with other kids around." He kept his voice light. "Why not just try and see?"

"Remind me," Sabrina said, still locking eyes with him. "How on earth did we get to be having this conversation?"

"You showed her the water," Mitch picked up on her tone and pulled her towards the laugh they'd share. "That's probably where you went wrong."

Her whole body softened when she laughed.

"She's beginning to understand. But I can't tell her too much at once," he told Annette.

In training, the body is pushed beyond its limits. It suffers, then reconstitutes itself. Muscles strengthen and develop a tolerance to lactic acid. Lung capacity increases. The heart grows in size. At the same time, understanding of the stroke accumulates. Young swimmers begin with a general impression, and move into the detail. As each new element is assimilated, the swimmer reaches a plateau, or even loses ground before progressing further. The mind too must remake itself.

Mitch swims the sets that he's written on the sandwich board for his faster swimmers: 500-metre warm-up. Pull 150 four times. Swim ten times 100 intervals. Kick for 500, then kick fifteen times 25 metres, intervals. Five hundred butterfly, five hundred choice. He's working his way one stroke at a time towards the finale, towards sprint 100, 75, 50, 25 with a fifteen-second recovery. These days, some of his swimmers are faster than he is.

He works hard enough that the air tastes very sweet when he gets to rest. Water rushes past his ears, his breath's bubbles burst around his face; each time his ears surface there's the gasp of his inhalation, the sudden emptiness of the air above the pool. When his hands meet the tile, another turn begins. The hands of the deck timer mark each second as it passes and sometimes, for length after length, he thinks of nothing at all, just feels the stroke.

Though not today. He's remembering that first time he saw the pool at Braeden Manor: no deep end, the water opaque, unused lane dividers tangled together at the far end. The windows along one side were almost obscured by the bushes and creeper growing outside. A faded sign pointed out that students who swam without a qualified lifeguard present did so at their own risk. He remembers how his heart lifted, how he almost cried when he saw it. Just the sight of the water, the thought of being immersed.

People evolved from fish. In the early weeks of pregnancy, the human embryo develops the beginnings of gills, which later become part of its ears. Air-breathing and lungs evolved in fish as a way of coping with oxygen-depleted waters. It makes perfect sense to Mitch that our brains and bodies carry traces of the distant, aquatic past, and this must account for the affinity some feel for water, for individuals with extraordinary skills. Those free-divers, for example: no one can really explain how they descend on a single breath six hundred feet below the surface, much less why they are drawn to sink to such lonely and dangerous depths. Yes, their lungs are more capacious than average, but even so, after fifty feet, they're compressed to all but nothing, and theoretically, after three or four minutes, all those divers should be dead. Some *do* die in their attempts, but most live... It's quite possible, Mitch thinks, that this is because they have retained some fishy capacities, some metabolic trick that scientists don't yet understand—and it's got to be the same for exceptional swimmers like Tara. They see the water and feel its pull; they know what to do because it's buried somewhere in the fish part of their brain.

He volunteered for 5:45 pickup in the mornings and said he could find another parent to drive Tara home after practice.

"All right, then," Sabrina said. Tara's arms were wrapped around her waist. "It's very kind of you to help. I can't promise, but we'll take you up on the month's free tryout."

That was it. A month later, Tara formally joined the Sharks: sixty swimmers from six to seventeen, their coach Mitchell McAllister, assisted by a series of university students and volunteers—brilliant, abysmal and everything in between. Jason, they decided, could manage the evening sessions. He could sit with his laptop and work while she trained. A bit of time out for you, Mitch pointed out to Sabrina.

"I don't particularly want that," she told him, but she returned his smile.

At the first meet, both parents leapt to their feet, yelling and cheering. At last, Mitch told Annette, they saw it:

how swimming against someone good could take four seconds off Tara's time; how close to each other, how grateful rivals can feel at the end of a hard race.

Soon Jason was asking questions about interval versus sprint and making up spreadsheets on his computer, to the point that Mitch had to rein him in. Though Sabrina, who had yelled just as loud, once came up to him at the coaches' bench where he was packing up his things, and said, "Thanks, Mitch. But this whole thing is weird. What the hell is it about?"

"Being in the water," he told her. He pointed out how Tara liked the fun stuff, too, water polo, the pyjama swim, all that. That she was not full of herself. Just *happy*. She was learning how to encourage those in the team who weren't sure they wanted to be there. The training and the competition, he explained, as they climbed the concrete steps and finally emerged from the fuggy, humid air into the late-afternoon sun, would provide her with many life lessons: How to decide what she wanted and work for it, short and long term. How to deal with setbacks. "Swimming is a way to find out who you are," he told Sabrina. She seemed to take it on, but she didn't often come to the meets after that.

Sabrina missed seeing Tara win the 200 breast, a stroke she'd learned from scratch with Mitch. It's all about timing, he'd told her: the amount of glide, the moment to pull the arms back, getting the kick and the reach to work together. You begin by thinking it through, but in the end, you learn to feel when it's right. In the pool that afternoon, Tara pushed a *v*-shaped wave of water ahead of her and overtook her rival in the first of eight lengths.

At the end, she gripped the rim of the pool, heaving for breath. Mitch, watching from the coaches' bench, knew that she'd be disqualified for not touching properly on her second turn. He watched the white-coated official zone in on Tara as she went to pick up her towel. The woman, hugely fat, squatted down to Tara's level, holding onto the railings for support. Quite a picture, the muscular little girl who knew how to part the water and pull herself through it with the minimum of wasted energy, the woman who had to drag the equivalent of another person wrapped around with her, day in, day out. On the face of it, Mitch thought, as he watched the thing play out, you'd say the wrong one is giving advice here, though the fact is, a lot of these amazing little swimmers end up as beached whales in middle age. Tara, he thought, would be bright enough to do the math. She was a great kid all round. She stood straight and looked the whale-woman in the eye. He wished he'd brought a camera with him.

Then she was there in front of him. Subdued, but no tears yet.

"DQ'd," she told him, looking to see how he took it. Her time, 1:22, would have been a meet record.

"Bad luck, great time!" He watched her break into a grin. Later, he'd explain to her that every disqualification is a gift, and that by the end of the season, she would have her time way further down; it was a given, really, if she just did what he asked of her, and kept on growing, which she surely would, and did.

Annette sold her business and began to come along on the meet weekends. She helped pack up the car, took photographs for the website, and looked after the younger swimmers, the girls especially. Once Sabrina had the twins and needed Jason home to help, it was often just the three of them in Mitch's car, making jokes, talking things over.

But the first two years were in some ways the best, because then all of it was so fresh, so very exciting. Tara qualified for Provincials with times almost two seconds faster than required. She would have been seeded first, but couldn't go because of a trip already planned to visit Jason's parents in Ontario.

"Of course that comes first," Mitch told Sabrina. They were in her kitchen; she'd invited him in for coffee when he dropped Tara off. "No problem," he said, raising his mug as if in a toast, and he more or less almost meant it. He saw her jaw relax as she let go of the fight she'd been preparing for, though the next morning at 5:45, Tara, red-eyed, was crying up boulders next to him in the car.

"I hate my parents!" she spat out as they turned into the freeway.

"Whoa!" He glanced across, then grabbed her shoulder for a moment. "They didn't know. And who pays for all this? Who brings you here, who washes your towels? All you've got to do is wait until next year."

"*Next year?*"

"Next year, you could be six seconds faster. You're eight," he told her. "You have nine more years of Provincials. Missing this one will save you from getting bored. And remember, you're part of a team. All this year, you'll be pulling the others after you and speeding them up, too." Actually, he was sure she'd be in the Nationals by twelve or thirteen.

And when she did get to her first Provincials, she beat all records and ended up with three gold medals, which she wore to the team dinner that night. The skin on her face looked taut, almost as if it had shrunk, and her eyes were very bright. She looked more like her mother, he thought. There was something otherworldly about both of them.

"I'm starving!" Tara told him as he passed by where she was sitting with her friend Alice and both of her parents. Sabrina had protested earlier about the unhealthy choice of restaurant but now she waved at him and seemed happy enough.

"Good to see you wearing your jewels," he told Tara.

"Did you get medals like these?" she asked.

"Not at your age, no," he told her. "I didn't get any hardware until I was much older than you."

"Why not?"

"I was never in a team at school," he said, moving on.

He had not always been Mitch, though there was no need for Tara to know that. He grew up under the name of Sebastian McAllister, in England, the only child of an actress and a history professor, who believed that from beginning to end, their son's school experience should be intellectually stimulating, rigorous, yet also creative and free. There was no need for Tara to know Mitch's story, but Annette had required detailed background information. Comprehensive life-story exchange had been part of the deal. And was quite probably worthwhile, he admitted once it was done.

"They were prepared to pay though the nose," he told her, "but nowhere was good enough." Sebastian, as he was then, attended four different elementary schools before ending up at Braeden Manor, a cutting-edge progressive secondary based in an Arts and Crafts–style mansion in Hampshire. It was famed for its dedicated staff, small classes and picturesque wooded environment. There were professional-quality art rooms and laboratories and a well-equipped theatre, in which, despite or because of his mother being an actress, he had absolutely no interest. Braeden was a boarding school, and by that time, he was happy enough to leave home.

Would he go for arts, languages, or sciences? Perhaps he'd prefer some middle ground between the three? Philosophy? What about the law?

Braeden's teachers were on first-name terms with their pupils, who were encouraged to create their own curriculum. There was endless freedom, provided it was something intellectual or artistic that you wanted to do, but the school was too small to field teams for any of the local leagues, and sports hardly figured at all. In any case, the feeling was that team games were warlike and suspect; the life of the mind was what they were there to explore, and the body figured only as an aesthetic object or the subject of scientific enquiry. Physical education took the form of recreational tennis and occasional runs over the fields, and tacked onto the side of one of the older buildings was a neglected 25-metre pool which students who knew how to swim were allowed to use, provided a waiver had been signed.

"That pool saved my life," Mitch told Annette on one of their early dates, a hike up the mountain. "They meant well, but it's tough having parents who ignore what you are. They wanted me in Oxford, never understood that books bored me, much less how I loved the water. By the time I got into swimming, I'd stopped telling them anything. There was the pool, and I was in it, timing laps, practising how to breathe, growing my shoulders. I got a book, *The Science of Swimming*, and worked from that. Can you imagine learning technique from a book? But it was a good book, and taught me everything. The strokes, how to train. I still think it's the best... I timed myself and kept a log. No one took much notice. Perhaps I'd like to make it into a science project? Well, perhaps.

"Poor grades saved me from Oxford, but university of some kind seemed unavoidable. I picked Bristol for its pool, and persuaded them to let me try out for the swim team. I wasn't quite good enough. If I'd started proper training and competed earlier, they told me, I'd have had a decent chance. Fuck this, I thought, it's my life. I went AWOL, took off, for years: Turkey, Thailand, India, Mexico, Australia, New Zealand..."

"I'd love to go to New Zealand," Annette said.

And maybe they would. Because it was getting to the point that he couldn't go on coaching, year on year, forever, and financially, a time would come when he would not have to. For a while now, he had had it in mind that he'd at least semi-retire in 2016. Go watch Tara in Rio and leave it at that, that's what he had been thinking.

The last part of the mountain trail was steep. They'd passed through old forest and he'd drifted away from where his story was going. In water, he told Annette, you learn yourself. Who you are. How far, how long you will go, what you think and feel as you set yourself on a course, just you and it. Water is always stronger than you, even when you're the best you can be, and if you make a mistake, it is waiting to fill you up. And if you're drunk, you shouldn't swim, especially in the dark, however warm the water and the air and however beautiful the glittering firmament above.

Between Sebastian and Mitch, he went by a variety of names. He had been that tanned guy picking grapes, selling sunglasses on the beach, or fish, or worse; he was the bloke running the little boat over to the island, or taking tourist money to see the turtles hatch. Also, he had been that guy passed out on the beach. He did the necessary to keep moving on from one sweet spot to the next, and at the same time he found his own way down and out of his own head. He sent only occasional postcards home.

By chance, Mitch arrived at Lake Taupo at the time of an open-water meet: a whole scene he had no idea about. Short-haul swimmers wear out fast, but he could still train for distance, and had been, informally, for years. So he took up open-water competition and for a while it gave a shape to his life: training, and saving for the race fees, and travel from one event to the next. And between races, he set out solo, crossed bays and straits, swam to distant islands, rested and returned. Though he still drank. But at least when he came to grief it was the in the Mediterranean, and not the North Sea. A yachtsman who'd done a lifesaving course fished him out.

"Chance in a million. I'd passed out, was probably a minute away from death. I remember him slapping my face, then going back to pump my chest some more. I vomited up half the ocean. And after that, I went home. My father was dead by then. Mum put me through detox and rehab: nine months, lord knows what it cost. I changed my name to Mitchell, and I met Laura, who brought me back to Vancouver. We lasted almost six years, and here I am now, five thousand miles away from where I began, on the Pacific Rim, coaching the swim team at the Fourth Street pool."

"What about your mother?" Annette asked. By then, they were sitting at the summit, the city, fields, islands and sea spread out below them; the sky intense cerulean, wisped with puffy clouds. Not a bad view to be sitting in, not at all.

"Annual visit and talk on the phone. She's forgetful now, lives in a retirement complex with helpers, and is lined up to move into care. She's never stopped calling me Sebastian. And the way she puts it is that I'm a teacher. She forgets the divorce and tells everyone, including me, that my Canadian wife and I live *near Vancouver*. Some things just stay out of shape and you have to let it be. It's about as good as you could expect." Mitch put his hand on Annette's shoulder, and she leaned into him. Her story, which had come first, was simpler: a father no man could live up to; difficulties with men who found her too assertive. One of the many things he liked about Annette was that she did not judge or argue with what he'd made of his own tangled experience. She didn't try to tell him what it all meant.

By the time the twins were toddlers, Tara's parents had put the property, with its lavender and baby vines, up for sale. Bad timing: it was on the market for years, but before Tara got to the Nationals, they managed to cut their losses and sell it to another set of hopefuls. They moved to the edge of town. Tara got to go to regular school. Jason had a job in IT but they were struggling financially.

"It sucks, but we just can't come," Sabrina told Mitch. Her voice was tight and he guessed she was holding back tears. "It's what to do with the twins and the cost of the flights out east." Annette offered to donate her flight to whichever parent most wanted to go; Sabrina said they'd be too embarrassed to accept.

"Really, they're splitting up," Tara told them on the way to the airport. She sighed, examined her hands in her lap. Mostly she looked older than twelve, though sometimes it went the other way.

"First Mom was bringing the twins to watch and Dad was staying home, then it was the other way around. Now they've sent Charlie and Louie to stay with Aunt

Karen so they can take the time to try and talk things through, just the two of them. I don't care." She glanced at him in the mirror, her ponytail whipping to the side as she moved her head.

"I guess you're better off without them around," Mitch said, "if all that's going on. That's probably what they think, too."

"No," she said, her voice wavering, "it's not. They just couldn't agree." He gripped the wheel as if to throttle it and managed to say nothing. Annette twisted right around and put her hand on Tara's knee.

"Well, kiddo," she said, "that sucks. But you know I have a very loud voice and I'd like your permission to cheer for three when you're on."

"Sure," Tara said. Her shoulders seemed to relax a little; she looked out the window. Planes were taking off and landing, and the runways shimmered in the heat. "Do we get a meal on the flight?" she asked, and Annette said no, but she had brought chicken pasta and banana bread in her carry-on.

At the hotel, Tara and Annette shared a room, leaving Mitch in a room on his own. Mitch barely slept, could only hope that Tara was drinking enough and visualizing, as he'd taught her to, each stroke of the race, every breath and every single turn, in real time. The feel of the water and the wall of the pool, the sounds, her time on the clock. It had been proved that the same neurons fired whether you were visualizing or swimming for real. You must make a memory of what you want to occur.

"You can either let stuff get to you," he told her when they said goodnight, "or you can say, 'None of that comes in the water with me.' Just swim."

A 6:30 warm-up. An hour and a half later, she appeared on deck sheathed in her turquoise-and-black kneeskin. She looked for him and Annette, gave them her thumbs-up salute, then, as soon as they'd returned it, looked back at the water and rolled her shoulders. She was about in the middle for height, Mitch noted. There were no real giants, no surprises. But he thought she looked pale. No, Annette said, it was the light, they all did except the black girl from Toronto in lane three. And they were all brilliant—he and Tara had studied the stats. This was where you met your match, which for the 100 free was Josie Georgeson, lane five, next to Tara in four: their times were a whisker apart. Across the board it was tight. The race was down to who wanted it most and had best accepted and nurtured that knowledge, fed and groomed it, let it take residence in their mind, day and night—but also on who had a bad day, not enough sleep, or too much going on at home.

"On your marks." Eight of them, strong, slim and streamlined in their racing suits, climbed up onto the diving blocks, adjusted their goggles and bent to grip the edge. What was she thinking? Of the water, the strokes ahead of her? Of nothing at all?

When the light flashed and the buzzer sounded, the swimmers sprang from the blocks, hung for a split second in the air, then sliced into the pool; they came up together. Buried in the crowd's roar, Mitch was counting her strokes, yelling Ra! Ra! Ra! and praying for the turn, because with this talent, a perfect or an imperfect turn would make the difference: arm, arm, tuck, kick up your butt, stay compact in the roll, feet slam the wall, push, rotate, *yes*! She surfaced half a length ahead of the rest. Mitch and Annette were on their feet with the worst of them, roaring as she came in almost a tenth of a second ahead. She yanked off her goggles to see her time. Mitch was in tears. It was not her fastest, but it was better than anyone else's and it had got her through. It was good to keep something in reserve. They worked their way down through the sea of parents and coaches.

"Cool!" she said.

"Very cool. Good work! You're well in," he said as Annette handed over the recovery drink; she nudged him and he backed off, managed not to say, in a choked voice, *I'm gonna be so proud of you.* Though as it turned out he was: two golds, one silver, and one bronze over a long three days, emotionally exhausting in the very best way. The pool and the hotel, the heats, finals, food, drink—it was as if nothing else existed. After dinner, they returned to the rooms and watched old Disney films. And then it was over, and they cracked jokes and gossiped all the way home.

When they got there, things changed. Jason did not appear. In the hall, Sabrina explained to Mitch and Annette that things had been falling apart since before the twins were born. She and Jason were pulling in different directions, couldn't agree on anything. It had always been that way to some extent and was even part of the attraction. Now, with the three kids, it wasn't possible anymore, not even bearable. Not for her. Counselling was useless. They were going to split. They were aiming to do everything fairly and with as little pain as possible. The twins would stay with Sabrina. Tara could choose where she wanted to live. Either way, there would be plenty of flexibility.

"I'm very sorry," Mitch told Sabrina. She grimaced, shrugged, turned away.

"I don't want to live with either of them!" Tara told Mitch when she called him later that night. "Can I come live with you and Annette? You guys are a such a lot of fun." And now he wonders: Supposing they'd said yes, sure, come right on over, we'll work it out somehow? Supposing they had taken her in? How might things have turned out then? But instead, he called Sabrina.

"Look," he said after he'd let her know what Tara wanted, "I'm just letting you know. If we can help in some way, please say, and of course we'll do what we can."

"I think we'll be fine, but thank you, Mitch," she replied. Did "we" include the kids? he asked Annette. Couldn't they have waited a bit, given how long they'd waited already?

Tara did not choose. She moved between the two homes. After six months, Jason decided to move to Toronto for work. He pointed out that it would make sense for Tara's training, if she wanted to come too, and by then, she did.

"She'll keep in touch," Annette reassured Mitch. He wasn't convinced, but she did. She called or Skyped pretty much every week, and wrote Mitch long emails packed with details about her training. They still got to watch her major events. She was in a documentary about young athletes, and on TV several times. Her new team practised in the Varsity Pool and at the Olympium, great 50-metre pools. School went well and she was being tipped for college scholarships. She was sixteen, and almost six feet tall, with the perfect swimmer's build. She kept her hair in a pixie cut, for convenience, she said, but it looked great on her. There had been two boyfriends, both swimmers, but neither relationship seemed intense or disruptive: they were probably too tired to get up to much, Annette thought.

After the move, Mitch found it uncomfortable running into Sabrina and the twins at the grocery store and realizing that in many respects he knew far more about her daughter than she did. There was that on his side, and something else on hers, a distance that seemed like restrained hostility. Did she think it was all his fault? Did she blame *swimming* for the breakup, or at least for the loss of her daughter? Blame *him,* in fact? Annette thought it very likely, though he hated to think that way. He'd always liked Sabrina. Still, it was Tara that mattered.

"The coaches here aren't any better than you, Mitch," she'd told him. "But the thing is, there are three of them."

"Well they must be doing something right," he pointed out. It was all going very well, come 2013.

It's properly bright outside now, almost time for the lifeguards and then the early swimmers to arrive, dropped off by whichever white-faced parent drew the short straw that day. And Mitch has swum the last sprint; he's feeling the workout, and he's had enough waiting. He just wants Tara to call as she promised she would, and he wants to say—well, what? He's said so many things in his head that now he doesn't know what's best, or even exactly what he thinks. He just wants to hear her voice. He goes, dripping, straight back to reception, and digs the phone out of his backpack.

Nothing. Doesn't she owe him some respect?

Kelly the receptionist gives him an odd look as she comes in and turns her screen on: semi-naked colleague dripping in the office.

"I'm going to get a coffee," he tells her, makes for the door, then returns for his shirt. During the five-minute drive he remembers something Tara said when she called a week ago with her news: Suppose I was pregnant, what would you think then? *I'd be fucking furious,* he'd thought.

"Well—"

"I'm not, by the way."

"Well, I'd be wanting to know how you felt about it...and to be honest, I'd be thinking, well, babies are great, but that is something you could do anytime over the next two decades."

He had wanted to say: *Look, sometimes it's hard to honour your gift, but you'll feel better for doing it in the long run.*

You'll never forgive yourself if you turn away now.

This is just a blip. Just hang in there a bit longer and it'll feel good again.

Hang in three more years. Get what you came for, then quit.

Why would you not do this?

You are so very, very lucky! How dare you throw your chance away!

But the thing was to handle it so that she didn't get backed into a corner. "Look," he said eventually, "It's a big decision. Just do this one thing for me. Take a week to think it over every which way one more time, then call me again."

She said yes.

So where is she?

He should get some breakfast, but can't decide what. He stirs cream and two sugars into a cup of strong coffee, carefully fits the lid to the cup, then drives back to the pool. He carries the coffee to the little outside area where there are picnic tables and some play equipment. He places the phone on the table about a foot away. I'll drink this, he thinks, and then I will either call her and say, *What the hell?* or smash this fucking phone with a rock. He enjoys the idea of the rock: it's ludicrous but that does not mean that he won't do it.

The taste of the coffee, its sweetness and temperature are perfect; he drinks slowly, pausing between mouthfuls to look at the pool building, the yellowing rhododendrons sprawled against it, the car parking area with its forlorn planters and lamps. He waits a little before taking the last mouthful. And then it's gone, and the phone rings.

"Hi, Mitch!" Her voice, light and even, gives no clue as to what she'll say. "You okay? Got a few minutes?" He doesn't mention that he should be at work.

"So, like you said, I've thought it over. "

"Great, Tara."

"Well, Mitch… I am a hundred percent certain that I'm not stressed. Or in love. And I've not over-trained. It's a fantastic programme and they switch things up a lot. And it's definitely not Max's or Roxy's or anyone's fault that I've come to feel this way. They're great coaches. I talked to them a few weeks ago, and they said to take a break and see if it freshened me up. I'm on my third week of the break now, and I really like it. I really, really like taking a break. And they sent me to a sports counsellor twice a week. Basically, I'm thinking, maybe I've swum enough?"

A counsellor once asked Mitch what the water represented for him and, when he said nothing, suggested it might be the womb.

"Tara—" he begins, but she doesn't stop for him.

"Of course, yes, there's the Big *O*. And the Pan Am. All these goals I've had, we've all had, for years. And it's been great to look forward to, but Mitch, my motivation's zilch. I've lost interest. In winning stuff. In the podium. It's like, done that."

But no, Mitch thinks, *you haven't! You've got very close, but turned away, which is a completely different thing*. He knows he's right. Also, that it is worse than pointless to say so. Tara's voice does not waver as she continues: "I don't *hate* it, as such, but I don't feel the pull anymore. You just can't train, you can't get there unless you really, really want what's at the end of it... I've changed. At first I ignored it, then I freaked out, but now it's fine, I think. Good, actually. Because why not? Why can't I be something different? I want to think about new things. The environment, stuff like that. And Mitch, it is so cool to pick up a book and not fall asleep by the end of the second page."

You have your whole life to read books!

She's still talking: how she might do volunteer work, and wants to see the world, not just the 50-metre pools in its major cities and the corridors of budget hotels. Could go to Guatemala. Bhutan. Thailand. Peru.

Beware of open water! Wear the life jacket!

She's thinking that when she's earned some money—*How?*—she'll make some long trips, journeys that include biking, kayaking and camping, but she'll also spend time in cities.

Always learn some of the language. Travel with someone. Buy your own drinks, and watch them!

"I feel awful about disappointing you all. But it is my life. I feel," Tara says, her voice growing slower and less certain, "like I've ended a very long swim. When you climb out of the pool and stand on dry land—you know that soft, heavy feeling while your body adjusts? And it is scary, because who am I without the water? What's left of me? I have no idea. But I want to know. And Mitch, I don't want to fall out over this. I really, really don't. Are you hearing me?"

He wants to advise her to at least keep her fitness up—after all, who is he to her if not her coach? He wants to tell her that in six weeks' or even six months' time, if she changed her mind, she could probably still come back. But he takes a deep breath and says none of it.

"Yes," he says and small as it is, that word comes hard, but then it's done. The tears that course down his face are a relief. "Loud and clear. Got it, Tara."

"Cool!" she says, her voice bright and free. "Thanks so much for everything, Mitch. I mean that. I'm heading west in a few weeks time. Guess I'll visit you guys then."

"All right, Tara. Take care."

It's over. He sits, head in hands, alone on the bench outside the pool, his swimmers inside waiting for him, his face wet: it's a strange feeling, a kind of passionate emptiness, an unexpected calm. Shock? Relief? Release? In any case, the best thing is to keep moving. Mitch stands, slips the cup in the trash and goes back in to the pool.

"It's just how and what it is, and good luck to her, but I can't pretend to like it," he tells Annette later, the pair of them folded into each other, pressed close, rocking back and forth.

"It could be the best thing ever for her." Annette pulls back a little so she can look up into his face. "And now, we have a truly empty nest... Please, Mitch, don't you dare turn us into a cliché. Let's go somewhere together, soon. Let's get away and start thinking about something else."

He has two weeks coming up. She's thinking about Iceland. It's mild and light almost all night long in August. You can cycle right round. It has puffins, geysers, hot springs, black beaches, all sorts of pools. You can scuba dive in the Silfra rift, swim in Viti lake.

Sure, Mitch says. It does sound great, though it's not cheap, and somehow they don't make the booking right away.

Then, about a week later, he glimpses Sabrina and the twins in the grocery store, ahead of him in the tea and coffee aisle, and it floods through him: how much she must have been through, how much she has had to let go. He catches up with her in produce, and asks her if she's heard from Tara. She nods and pulls a quick smile, meets his gaze.

"Apparently Jason took it very badly," she says. "But she said you were just great. Once she knows where she's going next, well, we all know she'll work hard for it." They're standing quite close. Her face is open, relaxed. He's not seen her like this before.

"I worry," Mitch finds himself saying, "that as time passes, she may miss the training routine itself far more than she expects."

"You could be right." Sabrina touches him on the shoulder and her hand rests there a second or two. "Mitch," she says, "when Tara gets back, we'll do dinner or something with you and Annette." Then she gathers up the twins and pushes her cart on towards the baked goods.

It's such a soft but sudden feeling—something like waking up, something like his first sight of the Braedan Manor pool or of Lake Taupo, something like déjà vu: the sensation of what used to be turning itself, in the space of a breath, into the beginning of something else.

Thanks & Acknowledgements

Crafting short stories is an oddly lengthy and very absorbing business. I offer heartfelt thanks to my husband and family, and to all at Biblioasis, especially to super-editor John Metcalf, and to the ever-patient Chris Andrechek in production. Acknowledgement for first publication is due to the *Walrus* for "The Last Cut" and "Red Dog," to *Carte Blanche* for "The Perfect Day," to the editors of *The Lighted Room* for "The Two of Us" (as "Rosemary"), to *Ars Medica* for "The Right Thing to Say," to *New Writing* for "It is July Now" and "Bees," and to *Numero Cinq* for "Open Water."

About the Author

RICHARD STEEL

Kathy Page's writing has been described as "compulsively readable" (*Time Out, London*) and ranges widely across genres. Her story collection *Paradise & Elsewhere* was nominated for the 2014 Giller Prize. She is the author of seven novels, including *Alphabet*, a Governor General's Award finalist in 2005, *The Story of My Face*, longlisted for the Orange Prize in 2002, and *The Find*, shortlisted for a Relit Award in 2011. She co-edited *In the Flesh* (2012), a book of personal essays about the human body, and has written for radio and television. Born in England, Kathy has lived on Salt Spring Island since 2001. For further information, please visit her website: www.kathypage.info.